PENNY'S YULETIDE WISH

PENNY'S YULETIDE WISH

A BRANCHES OF LOVE NOVELLA

SALLY BRITTON

BLUE WATER BOOKS

ALSO BY SALLY BRITTON

The Inglewood Series:

Book #1, *Rescuing Lord Inglewood*

Book #2, *Discovering Grace*

Book #3, *Saving Miss Everly*

Book #4, *Engaging Sir Isaac*

The Branches of Love Series:

Prequel Novella, *Martha's Patience*

Book #1, *The Social Tutor*

Book #2, *The Gentleman Physician*

Book #3, *His Bluestocking Bride*

Book #4, *The Earl and His Lady*

Book #5, *Miss Devon's Choice*

Book #6, *Courting the Vicar's Daughter*

Book #7, *Penny's Yuletide Wish*

Forever After:

The Captain and Miss Winter

Timeless Romance:

An Evening at Almack's, Regency Collection 12

Entangled Inheritances:

His Unexpected Heiress

For My Grandfather
"Merry Christmas."

R obert Ellsworth's entrance to the haberdashery made the bell above the door jingle merrily, alerting the shopkeeper and his assistant. Robert closed his umbrella before fully entering and dropped it in the small barrel near the door. Despite the mud-filled streets, Mr. Clyde's floor was as neat as ever, which made Robert hesitate to come fully inside.

"Ah, Mr. Ellsworth. Come in, come in." Mr. Clyde himself stood behind the counter, beaming at Robert. "Have you come for your gloves?"

"I have, Mr. Clyde. Are they ready?" Robert came further in, keenly aware of the mud on the heels of his boots. Despite the cold drizzle, he had spent most of his morning walking from one end of the village to the other on errands for his employer.

A young man stuck his head out between the curtains separating the front of the shop from the back. "Is that Mr. Ellsworth?"

"Yes, Rollins. Bring his gloves out. Look smart, lad."

All the town's gentlemen went to the haberdashery for gloves, and oftentimes it was just the place for them to obtain other odds and ends. Robert had been measured for new leather gloves the week before.

The apprentice hatter brought out the black gloves and handed them to Mr. Clyde, but the older man shook his head. "No, Rollins. You did the work. You present them."

Robert's heart sank slightly, but he kept a cheerful smile upon his face. No use discouraging the lad. It wasn't Rollins's fault that a mere steward might accept the work of someone new to the trade while an established gentleman could expect more consideration from the proprietor.

The boy's work, when Robert examined the gloves, looked well enough. When he put the gloves on, they fit snuggly and he could open and close his fingers without straining the seams. "Well done, Mr. Rollins." He looked the young man directly in the eyes as he paid the sincere compliment. "They're as fine a pair of gloves as I have ever worn before."

The boy's ears turned pink and he bowed slightly. "I am pleased to hear it, Mr. Ellsworth." Robert paid the agreed-upon price, then added a few extra coins for the young man. He began to turn away from the counter when Mr. Clyde cleared his throat.

"Mr. Ellsworth, I wonder if you might know—does Mr. Devon have need of our services before he goes to London for the Season?"

Robert maintained his cheerful demeanor. "I do not know, sir. Nothing in the house books indicates one way or the other if the family will make clothing purchases before leaving." The question was far beneath his position, yet he well understood Clyde's desire to secure business before the wealthier members of the community left for the larger town and shops. He took up his umbrella from the barrel, flexed his hands in the new gloves, and stepped outside.

The rain had let up for the moment. Without knowing how long the sky would grant such a reprieve, Robert moved at a hurried pace down the lane. Since early December, the weather had been biting cold and wet. There were talks of flooding in other parts of the county and in London itself. The deluge was unusual for the season, and no one had been prepared for it.

At least most crops were in. Mr. Devon's lands were high enough that the water did not settle in his fields, and the tenants' cottages were newly built and free from leaks and drafts, which meant Robert had little to trouble his duties in relation to the weather.

A fat drop of rain fell past the tip of his nose, and another off the brim of his hat. Grumbling to himself about the state of the roads, Robert rushed to raise his umbrella before him and slid it open.

A startled exclamation made him hastily move the umbrella upward.

"I beg your pardon—" The apology died upon his lips when his eyes took in the woman before him, her large golden-brown eyes widened in her surprise. One red-gloved hand rested over her chest, as though to calm her heart. Deep brown curls peeked out from beneath her emerald-green bonnet.

"Penny." The childhood name fell from his lips as soft as a prayer. "What are you doing here?"

Her eyes narrowed and her lips parted as though she wanted to correct the familiarity, but swiftly the expression cleared, and her bright smile appeared.

"Robert, is that you? Oh, I cannot believe it." She held out the same hand that had been pressed over her heart.

He took it in his own, a tingle dancing up his fingers as they came in contact with hers, despite both of them wearing gloves. He bowed over her hand, careful to keep the umbrella from assaulting her a second time. "It is wonderful to see you." He straightened after she curtsied. "Whatever are you doing in Annesbury? I never thought to see you here again."

Her gaze dropped to the ground. "My aunt has come to visit an old school friend. Since this is where my brothers and I spent our childhood, she invited me to come, too. We are staying with Mr. and Mrs. George Brody." She peered up at him from beneath the brim of her bonnet. "I am glad to find you here. I did not know whether you were still in the neighborhood. I heard about your father's passing. I am sorry for that, Robert."

"Thank you." Robert's father had passed away in the spring, after fighting a long illness that had left him often confused and weak. Robert's heart clenched at the memory of his father's last days, of how hopeless and gray things had been. He cleared his throat and forced a smile upon his face. "How long will you visit?"

Penny accepted the change of topic gracefully, raising her head and presenting him with a brighter beam. "A fortnight. We will be here through January seventh."

"Ah, all twelve days of Christmas." Robert shifted his weight from one foot to the other, wishing it had actually started raining. The drops he felt before had been alone in their journey from above, so now he appeared somewhat foolish. Closing the umbrella might only draw attention to that fact, however, so he kept it above him. "I will make a point of visiting. I imagine there are many in the neighborhood who will be happy to renew their acquaintance with you."

"I doubt many remember me." Her hand fluttered by her side as though to brush away the idea of anyone having missed her.

But Robert had missed her. He thought of her every time he passed the pond where they had skipped rocks, and when he glimpsed her favorite marigolds growing in a neighbor's garden or when he saw the small scar on the palm of his hand from where he'd slipped and fallen out of a tree they had climbed together. That meant he thought of her at least once a day.

Since she and her brothers had gone to be raised by her aunt and uncle, he had not stopped wondering how she had fared. He had often thought of writing, but never worked up the courage. What did a boy of seventeen have to write to a girl of fifteen? A girl who had lost her parents and her home?

To have her standing before him again, more beautiful than he remembered, made Robert's heart swell up so that it nearly choked him.

A childhood fondness should not affect him in such a way.

"I will be at the Earl of Annesbury's famous Christmas ball tomorrow evening," she informed him when he had been quiet too long.

Robert forced himself to speak, to keep his tone light. "Wonderful. My brother and I received invitations as well." He ought to ask her to dance. Secure her hand for the supper dance, or a waltz, or an entire set. But how presumptuous of him, to think she would wish such a thing when they had not seen each other in years. "We will see one another tomorrow evening, then."

If she did not think him a dolt before, she certainly would after.

A mischievous light kindled in her eyes, a light he knew well from their childhood adventures together. "We had better, Mr. Ellsworth. When we do, I expect you to ask me to dance." She curtsied and he bowed instinctively, putting an end to their conversation.

A scent of cinnamon teased his nose as she walked around him, her pink lips curved upward as though she held a secret. She was probably laughing at him.

Then she was gone, her deep green spencer cut in such a way to emphasize the pleasing curves of her form. He watched as she joined an older woman at the door of a shop, the two of them linking arms before they continued down the street.

Penny's head started to turn, as though she would look over her shoulder at him, and Robert hastened to walk away before she caught him staring.

Penelope Clark had returned to the neighborhood, and she had changed from the trim, freckled girl of his acquaintance—a childhood playmate—to a woman grown. Yet he had known her the instant their eyes met, recognized the girl he had cherished and adored throughout their friendship.

At least he had never told her, never worked up the courage as a youth, to tell her the truth of his feelings. Robert's hesitation on that point had surely saved him from humiliation. All for the best. After all, the loss of her parents took Penny and her brothers away; and the loss of his father forced him into employment as a steward, a position far beneath what most gentlemen's daughters would accept in a future husband.

Robert struck that thought away. Connecting the idea of marriage to Penny would only lead to disappointment.

CHAPTER 2

Penny slipped her arm through that of her Aunt Elizabeth's and looked over her shoulder. She caught one last glimpse of Robert as he hurried down the street, umbrella open and overhead even though there were no more raindrops to harry the people out of doors.

They entered the bakery where Mrs. Brody had completed placing their order of a Twelfth Night cake. The warmth of the cozy shop made Penny realize how cold her face and fingers had become in her walk down the village streets.

Mrs. Brody, her aunt's kind friend, turned to them both, her expression as welcoming and cheery as ever. "Well, Miss Clark? Have you found much changed since your time living in Annesbury?"

Robert had certainly changed. He'd grown taller, and handsomer. She kept that to herself, however. "Some of the shops have new coats of paint, signs have changed, but so much is as I remember it."

"I am glad to hear you find it familiar," Mrs. Brody

said, her tone gentle. "I have completed my errands. Do either of you have things you need to do while in the village?"

Aunt Elizabeth and Penny could not think of a thing, so the three ladies exited the shop and walked to the waiting carriage to return to the Brody estate. Mrs. Brody led the way, and once they had all climbed inside and settled with blankets upon their laps, Aunt Elizabeth took it upon herself to begin the conversation in a most unexpected manner.

"Penelope, who was that gentleman you were speaking to upon the street? I did not glimpse more than his back, but you seemed in rather animated conversation."

Mrs. Brody's eyebrows raised, too. "Oh, a gentleman? Have you already found yourself an admirer, Miss Clark?" Mrs. Brody had a great deal of playfulness about her, the sort that immediately made her endearing to those not too high in the instep.

"Dear me. An admirer after less than a quarter hour in the village." Penny laughed and raised her eyes to the heavens, sighing wistfully. "If only it were so easy to attract a gentleman." Perhaps she would have been married were such the case. Yet she could not find it in herself to bemoan her state as an unwed maiden. Not now. Not after seeing Robert. "It was Robert Ellsworth, to answer your question. He and I grew up together. My parents were the very best of friends with his, and we were as often in each other's company as not."

She had adored him in their childhood and missed him terribly when she went away. Losing her parents had been the worst moment in her life. Losing Robert had caused nearly as much pain. Her only consolation had been keeping her brothers with her.

Mrs. Brody shared a knowing glance with Aunt Elizabeth. Were they both planning to matchmake now? "Oh, he is a very fine gentleman. Most polite. Good family. His elder brother, Mr. Samuel Ellsworth, is the head of that family now. Robert has taken a position with the Devon family, as land steward."

Penny leaned back in her seat. "A steward? For the Devons?"

Mrs. Brody was quick to assuage Penny's surprise. "The younger Mr. Devon, of course. His sister, Christine, and my brother are married." Ah, yes. The elder, somewhat frightening Mr. Devon had died a few years previous. Penny remembered that bit of local history with relief. How had Robert come to be a steward? He had been determined, once upon a time, to take up the law.

"Robert was always very responsible. I imagine he excels in his position." Penny folded her hands in her lap and turned her attention to the window, permitting her Aunt Elizabeth and Mrs. Brody to converse on matters familiar to them both, enjoying their old friendship.

Penny relaxed into her seat, grateful the attention no longer rested on her. She could entertain her thoughts in peace for a moment. Robert had looked well. Had he wed? She ought to have asked Mrs. Brody but dwelling on him as a conversation topic might give Aunt Elizabeth the wrong idea. Her aunt had become rather determined to matchmake, in order to prevent Penny from following through on her idea to find a position as a schoolteacher.

Aunt Elizabeth and her husband, Uncle Matthew, had only ever been kind and generous. They were not the relations one read of in storybooks, forcing orphaned children to live in cellars or drafty attics. They had purchased a commission for her eldest brother when he expressed interest in the military and had assisted the next brother in attending Edinburgh to pursue a career in medicine. For Penny, they had brought in tutors of every sort she could wish—for art, music, language studies. She had turned into a very accomplished young woman, if she did say so herself.

They even increased her dowry from the respectable two thousand pounds her father had left her to four thousand pounds. It was enough to reassure suitors, but not enough to attract any in its own right. Which explained why Penny, an orphan with no connections in Society, remained unmarried.

She sighed as raindrops started to splatter against the window. The carriage might become mired if they did not make better speed. The trip to visit the Brodys had taken three times what it should have, due to the conditions of the smaller, connecting roads. What an adventure that had been, climbing from the carriage to assist in pushing it out of a particularly mucky rut.

"Of course, there is the earl's ball tomorrow," Aunt Elizabeth said, nudging Penny with her elbow.

Penny brought her attention back to her aunt. "I do apologize, aunt. What were you saying about the ball?"

Mrs. Brody chuckled. "I was telling your aunt we ought to find you a few suitable young people to keep you entertained. I know we cannot possibly hold your interest for a fortnight."

"Then I suggested the ball as a wonderful place to find you a few friends," Aunt Elizabeth added. "Within moments of arriving here, I was informed that everyone who is anyone goes to the ball."

Penny was not anyone. Not at all. Her parents had held a respectable place in Annesbury, but they had leased the estate where they lived and did not have an enormous fortune to leave their children upon their sudden, unexpected deaths.

The way her aunt's eyes narrowed and took on an especially troubling gleam told Penny there was the possibility of matchmaking at this ball as well. It took a great deal of willpower to not comment upon her aunt's intentions. Aunt Elizabeth only wanted to see Penny happy, of course, and so had not yet admitted defeat. But at twenty-four years old, Penny had quite given up on making an advantageous match. She would rather find happiness and love than convenience, and she could support herself in the interim.

But she put those concerns away for the moment, thinking instead of the ball. Hopefully, Robert would ask her to dance.

CHAPTER 3

Christmas morning, Robert arrived at his brother's home on horseback. He'd ridden rather than attempt to make his way by carriage. He'd had his finer clothes for the evening sent over the day previous, so luggage was of no concern. The ride had been easy and fairly pleasant as he rode in naught more but a light drizzle, a drizzle his overcoat and hat protected him from well enough. Yet he remained agitated.

It seemed that his brother had noticed. Samuel, seated before the parlor's great fire with a pipe in one hand and a book in the other, looked over the cover at Robert. "Something troubling you, Rob?"

"No," Robert answered hastily, straightening his waistcoat. "What makes you ask such a thing?"

Their youngest brother, home for a holiday from Harrow, piped up from his chair and desk where he was sharpening a pen in a questionable manner. "You keep going to the window, looking out, and sighing as though there are weighty matters on your mind."

Robert stepped away from the window. "I apologize. I did not realize I was behaving so distractedly."

The book in Samuel's hand snapped when he closed it abruptly. "Now he apologizes for acting strangely yet resists explaining matters to us. You can see, there, by the set of his shoulders that he has no intention of sharing his woes."

"Ah, I do see." Peter nodded in a manner more fitting to an aged, wise man than a seventeen-year-old school-boy. "We ought to torture it out of him, obviously."

Though the matter on his mind weighed no less heavily, Robert laughed and folded his arms across his chest. "I should like to see you try, pup." Quick as a wink, Samuel's book was gone and he'd launched himself at Robert, wresting his arms behind his back. "The pup has a guard dog, brother."

Robert laughed more than he struggled. It had been ages since the three of them had engaged in any kind of tussle. It had felt wrong, since their father's death, to have moments of lightness between them.

Peter came forward with his feathered pen and waved it beneath Robert's nose. "Now we shall torture you in truth, Robert." He let the tip of the feather brush Robert's chin. "What has you so out of sorts this fine Christmas morning? The service was short." He tickled Robert's nose, making it itch. Robert stood firm, refusing to fight his way free. Withstanding the feather would not be difficult.

"I am not out of sorts."

"Another denial," Samuel said jovially. "Give him what for, Peter."

Robert's nose was subjected to a fierce attack of feather thrusts, causing it to itch, wrinkle, and then—

His sneeze shook the clock on the mantel, he was certain of it. Peter had wisely removed himself from the trajectory of the blast, and Samuel laughed harder. "Still susceptible, I see. After all these years." He released Robert's arms in time for Robert to emit a second sneeze, as loud and large as the first.

"That will teach him to withhold information from us." Peter's words were well-colored by smug amusement. "Now you must tell. Those are the rules."

Those blasted childhood rules. The boys had invented them when Peter had barely come out of leading strings. There was always a forfeit to be paid if one of them succumbed to the childhood tortures they devised, whether it was arm-wrestling, a coin toss, or the feather torture. The rules held.

Robert pulled his waistcoat and then the sleeves of his coat back into place. "You are both terribly wanting in propriety and maturity. I want that made clear." When Peter and Samuel only stared at him, wearing nearly identical smirks, Robert released an aggravated groan. "Very well. If you must know, I met with an old friend yesterday. By chance. It has left me distracted."

"An old friend?" Samuel asked. "Pray tell, what is this old friend's name?"

For an instant, Robert considered refusing to tell, but Peter still twirled the offensive feather in his fingers. He answered with resignation. "Penelope Clark."

Peter's eyebrows drew together in confusion, but Samuel rocked backward on his heels. "Ah. Frederick's sister." Frederick was the second son of the Clark family, and the one who had been of an age with Samuel when their family lived at the neighboring estate.

"I still do not understand," Peter complained, lowering his hands to his side. "A girl?"

"A woman by now, I should suspect," Samuel said, sounding as though he had grown thoughtful. "In bygone days, Miss Clark and Robert were thick as thieves. You must remember her, though it was seven years ago her family left."

The boy apparently considered this a moment. "Was she that girl Robert always ran about with during the summer? Penelope—we called her Penny. Yes." Recognition dawned on his face, as did a big grin. "I remember now."

Robert made his way back to the safety of his armchair and dropped in it heavily. "Her aunt has a friend in the neighborhood. Penny—Miss Clark, I should say, is visiting the Brodys with her aunt."

"And a visiting friend has you staring at the window like you are contemplating the finer points of philosophy," Peter said, sounding disgusted.

Samuel laughed, shortly. "I imagine it's more the poets Rob is considering at the moment."

"I haven't any idea what you mean." Robert let his head fall back against the chair, directing his gaze to the ceiling rather than to his brothers. "I was merely thinking upon all that she must have gone through since the loss of her parents." Perhaps that comment would sober his brothers' wit.

"Interesting." Samuel walked back to his corner of the couch and took up his pipe before taking his seat. "I would not think such a morose thought would cause you agitation. Tell us more about your meeting with Miss Clark, Robert. How is she, after all these years? Did she look well?"

"She appeared to be in excellent health," Robert answered right off, though the memory of her brightened eyes and pink-lipped smile made heat rise into his ears. "And she seemed happy." Radiant, actually. She had seemed radiant.

Samuel puffed on his pipe another moment, and Robert could see Samuel's speculative look from the corner of his eye. "Happy. I suppose that is good news. Did you speak to her long or only in passing?"

"In passing." Robert sat up in his chair and picked up a book on the nearby table, not even paying attention to the title before opening it to a page somewhere near the middle. "We hardly spoke at all, in fact."

"But you spoke enough to determine she is yet unmarried?" Samuel asked.

Despite his attempt to remain calm, Robert's gaze flew from the page. "She is—" But he had not asked. She had not revealed anything about her marital state. Would she not have corrected his use of her Christian name if she were married? She would not go about the countryside making extended visits with her aunt if she had a husband of her own to look after. At least, he did not think she would.

"You do not know," Peter breathed, sounding somewhat awed. "Oh. I begin to understand the situation."

Then Peter understood more than Robert. "There is no situation." Robert made a show of turning the page, though he had not read a single word of the first.

"You like her," Peter said. "He does, doesn't he?" The boy looked to their eldest brother for confirmation.

Robert said "no" at the same moment Samuel said, "It seems so."

Hurriedly, Robert amended his statement. "Of course, I like her in terms of friendship. We had always been friends until she left to live with her relatives."

Peter and Samuel exchanged a knowing glance. Samuel spoke slowly. "How long will she be in the area?"

"A fortnight." Robert turned another page and tried to indicate by his posture alone that the subject had closed.

"Ah. Then we must pay Miss Clark and her esteemed aunt a call. Or perhaps they will be at the ball this evening."

Though he had to bite his tongue to keep from answering, Robert remained silent on the matter. He tried to read something from the book in his hands and realized he had somehow found a slim volume of poetry, almost confirming Samuel's earlier words about his preoccupation with the poets. Robert gritted his teeth together.

The memory of Penny's gold-flecked eyes, wide with surprise, surfaced once more. If she had married, he could not think of her with the affection stirring in his breast, and he ought not think of her at all until he knew. Not that it mattered. Even if Penny had never married, even were she free to flirt, court, and wed a man, he could not count himself worthy of her.

Had he a career in the law, property of his own, there would be a chance. A land steward had no right to wed a woman such as she, someone who deserved all the comforts and securities of a large income and a husband who did not have to work for another to provide a living to her.

It did not matter that his heart leaped upon recognizing her. At least she did not know how deep his feelings ran, that the last time he saw her before returning to school, before she lost her family, he had made up his mind to one day wed her.

A boy's love was not the same as a man's. He had to put it behind him. They were, and could only ever be, friends.

CHAPTER 4

In her favorite red silk dress, with a sprig of holly tucked artfully in her hair and white pearls taking the place of mistletoe, Penny stared at her reflection with narrowed eyes. The last time she wore her gown to a ball, she had walked with confidence and never thought her looks wanting. Some gowns made her feel pretty, but this one made her believe that someday there might be someone who found her beautiful.

For the first time, she found herself eager to see the reaction of a gentleman when he spied her in the red dress. Robert's opinion on her appearance had started to matter the year she turned fifteen. She had changed the way she wore her hair, took more care in choosing the design of her clothing, all with an eye for trying to please her dearest friend. Of course, he had been oblivious, as most boys of that age would be.

But they were not children anymore.

"Penny?" her aunt called from the corridor. "Are you ready, my dear? The carriage is at the door."

Penny worried her bottom lip between her teeth, causing it to darken. She swept up her black cloak and fan, then hurried out of the room. "I am coming, Aunt." She sailed down the staircase, her stomach twisting and turning with more than excitement.

Her aunt and uncle stood at the bottom of the stairs, Mr. and Mrs. Brody with them, and the Brody's eldest daughter, Miss Alice Brody, already wrapped in her royal purple cloak.

"Oh, Miss Clark," the Brody's daughter exclaimed, her blue eyes sweeping over Penny's gown. "You are absolutely stunning. I wish I were permitted to wear red."

Penny hesitated on the last step. Many considered red a bold color, not meant for young, unmarried women. It was not innocent, maidenly, or modest to draw attention in such a way. Yet she was not a girl at her coming-out ball. At her age, Penny could wear what she wished. The red suited her. She made up her mind. "I thank you, Miss Brody. I confess, this gown's color gives me great confidence in my enjoyment of the evening."

"A seventeen-year-old girl ought to content herself with a white gown and gold sash," Mrs. Brody said to her daughter with a raised eyebrow. Then she turned to Penny, and her gentle smile returned. "You look lovely, my dear."

"I agree. The holly was a perfect touch." Aunt Elizabeth studied the gown another moment, then took Penny's cloak to help wrap it around her shoulders. "We must go, else we will be late."

The butler opened the front door, and the six of them flitted down the steps. Straw had been scattered from the last step of the house to the carriage and all the way down the drive to help them make it to the road without getting stuck in the mud. It had been a near thing in order to attend services that afternoon. The local vicar held morning and afternoon services on Christmas Day, with most choosing to attend one or the other. The Brodys had preferred the afternoon. Apparently, Mr. Robert Ellsworth and his brothers had preferred the morning.

Not that Penny had spent a great deal of time looking for them. The Brodys sat near the front of the throng, and to look for Robert would have meant stretching her neck about like a goose to look over her shoulder.

The sky hung heavily above them, black with night and clouds, but the coach had its lanterns and a servant rode ahead with a lamp. They were safe enough, even in the darkness. The earl's estate was not far.

"I was too young to attend any of the balls when we left Annesbury," Penny remarked, not to anyone in particular. "I have heard they are magical."

"Indeed, they are. And there is always something that happens to surprise us. One year, it was the earl himself announcing my brother's engagement to his wife," Mrs. Brody said, following the remark with a laugh.

Mr. Brody joined his wife in the merriment, also enjoying the memory of that evening. "Betrothals do tend to be announced at these events. Last year it was Mr. Horace Devon to the vicar's daughter, Margaret Ames. Miss Clark, were you at all acquainted with Miss Ames? I believe you two are of an age."

"She was a few years younger than me," Penny admitted. "And the vicarage was on the other side of the village from where I lived." Which was one of the reasons why she was not overly familiar with the Devon family. She hoped the younger Devon proved a kinder employer than his father. It would pain her to learn Robert worked for a less than amiable man.

"It would be so romantic to be present for a wedding announcement," Miss Brody murmured, her sigh slipping through the darkness to underscore the words.

A long time ago, Penny had thought the same. But her parents died in November the year she turned seventeen, just before she would have attended the ball for the first time, and there were no grand gatherings for her for a year afterward. By the time she went to her first ball, it was in her uncle's village, and she had been too shy to attract the attention of gentlemen wishing to dance.

After she grew out of her shyness, Penny typically did not see the romance of such an evening. It was all well and good to dress in one's finest clothes and spend hours speaking to friends, enjoying refreshments and the company of one's neighbors, but the gentlemen had never quite appealed to her. Possibly only because she did not quite appeal to them. No connections. No fortune. Not enough beauty to attract attention through looks alone.

Yet that night, knowing she would be among the people of Annesbury, and that she would see Robert in particular, her practicality had abandoned her and left excitement in its place.

When their carriage pulled up to the wide, stone steps leading to the main doors of the earl's grand house, Penny's heart thrummed rapidly against her chest. Would Robert have arrived already? There were dozens of carriages along the walk, pulled to the side, their drivers chatting and caring for horses.

Robert might be present, inside, perhaps watching for

her arrival. She entered the large house, and a servant took her cloak before ushering the ladies in their party to the retiring room where maids waited to assist with fixing hair arrangements and other women exchanged half-boots for dancing slippers. Penny paced from the door to where her aunt and Mrs. Brody sat, taking their time, conversing with another woman Penny did not immediately recognize.

"Penelope, dear." Her aunt took Penny's hand. "Do you remember Mrs. Thomas Gilbert? She is Mrs. Brody's sister-in-law."

"Oh." Recognition broke upon her, and Penny made a hasty curtsy. "Mrs. Gilbert, your family raises horses."

"Among other things," Mrs. Gilbert said, her eyes dancing with good humor. "At the moment, I feel more as though I am raising a pack of wild animals."

Before Penny could voice her confusion, Mrs. Brody laughed. "Christine, you cannot call three sons a pack of wild animals. I have seven children, as wild as yours, but they are all angels, no matter what mischief they might stir up."

Mrs. Gilbert huffed, but her smile was genuine enough in the very next instant. "You say angels, I say wild creatures. I doubt Miss Clark wishes to hear this old argument." She gave her attention back to Penny. "It is good to see you again, Miss Clark. Might I ask after your brothers?"

Though Penny wanted nothing more than to escape the retiring room and have a look around for a certain gentleman, she answered Mrs. Gilbert's pointed question, and then another, and another, until half a dozen of them had been posed to her and each answered as politely as she knew how. It seemed to take ages for Mrs. Gilbert to release her, and even then, she exchanged still more pleasantries with Mrs. Brody and Aunt Elizabeth. Penny's dancing slippers nearly tapped impatiently of their own accord.

At last her aunt stood and announced she was ready. Penny took her arm and the two of them followed Mrs. Brody. Uncle Matthew and Mr. Brody had waited to escort their wives up the stairs and to the receiving line. The earl and his countess greeted all their guests together, and a rather handsome young man stood at the countess's side.

Mr. Brody bowed and then made the necessary introductions. "My lord, my lady, might I present our dear friends Mr. and Mrs. Matthew Marham, and their niece, Miss Penelope Clark." After bows and curtsies were exchanged, the countess gestured to the young man at her side.

"Miss Clark, allow me to introduce my son, Phillip, Baron Heatherton. He is taking a brief respite from his studies at Oxford." Phillip, likely several years Penny's junior, made a proper bow and engaged her in conversation while the married couples exchanged pleasantries. "It is a pleasure to meet you, Miss Clark. Are you familiar with our part of the country?"

"I am. I lived here, as a matter of fact, until seven years ago. My family leased Glennwood for several years."

"Ah, that would put you quite out of my set, then." He offered her a charming smile, obviously meaning no disrespect. "I was a schoolboy when your family lived here. It is a pleasure to meet you on more even ground now. Would you grant me the privilege of saving me a dance, Miss Clark? I should like to hear about where you have been since leaving Annesbury."

The boy had perfect manners. "I would be honored, my lord."

"The honor is mine." He bowed again, at the same moment her uncle and aunt moved away toward the ballroom. She curtsied and took her leave, gripping the fan hanging at her wrist tightly enough that it creaked in her grasp.

As silly as it might be, Penny anticipated Robert's expression when he saw her with curiosity. Would he think her pretty? Of course, it would not matter if Penny happened to see him with a wife upon his arm. She had never found a way to ask if the Devon steward had married or remained unattached. They were only friends.

Yet the thought of a woman upon his arm, a woman with the privilege of belonging to Robert, made her remember the keen feeling of jealously she had experienced years ago, when Robert had walked another young lady home from church. The fact that the memory, along with the emotion, came back without warning made something inside her tighten most unpleasantly.

Try as she might, putting that memory away took several moments of concentration.

The earl's grand estate boasted a dedicated ballroom, with a balcony full of musicians tuning their instruments. The dancing had not begun, though the room was filled to bursting with people dressed in their finest attire, and everywhere Penny looked she saw the decor had been chosen quite obviously with a winter theme in mind. The floor had been chalked with snowflakes of silver and blue, and ribbons in matching colors were tied and looped around every column. Green boughs and wreaths covered the walls with ice-blue ribbons and silver bells adorning them. There was even a tree at the far end, such as the royal family were purported to have in the palace, festooned with silver and gold candles.

Snowflakes of delicate lace hung from thin threads above the crowd, as though falling from the ceiling. The whole effect was quite marvelous, especially considering that the weather made it unlikely real snow would fall anytime soon.

Aunt Elizabeth gestured for Penny to join her. "Dear me, Penelope. Have you ever seen so many kissing balls?" She fluttered her fan in the direction of the ceiling.

"I had not spied any." Penny looked up and saw, hanging amidst the snowflakes and beneath the musician's balcony, a green ball with silver-colored berries upon it. The decorations and lights nearly hid the ball from view, but apparently enough young ladies had noticed it so that no one stood beneath. One would have to stretch their arms quite high to come near to plucking a berry from it.

"They are everywhere beneath the balconies." A long walkway was above the ballroom floor on one side, allowing for chaperones to stand upon it and look down at dancing couples. Not many people stood near the rail at that moment. Beneath that walkway, kissing balls hung at regular intervals, nearly hidden by ribbons and wreathes. On the other side of the room, a few of the doors leading outside also had the treacherous decor waiting to trap poor maidens into kisses.

"Whatever must the countess be thinking?" Uncle

Matthew said, a sly grin upon his face. "I wonder if that son of hers put her up to it."

Mrs. Brody had been standing nearby, listening to the conversation. "I imagine it is the earl's doing. Everyone knows that Lord Annesbury is a tad eccentric." She gestured to the far side of the room where several chairs lined the walls. "Come, Elizabeth. I should like to introduce you to my brother, Thomas."

Though Penny had kept her eyes roving along the walls and through the crowds, she had yet to spy Robert. Following her aunt somewhat reluctantly, she tried not to be too disappointed. Not everyone had arrived yet, after all.

But then, even if Robert did not come at all, Penny still meant to enjoy herself.

CHAPTER 5

M usic streamed out of windows which were barely cracked to allow for the night air to cool the crowded ballroom. Robert tried to walk faster, realizing the dancing had started. Samuel had made them late, lingering over their dinner and then in conversation with Peter. Though they were not the only carriage still unloading before the earl's estate, Robert wished they had been among the first rather than among the last to arrive.

Try as he might to tell himself he had no right to take up Penny's time, he could justify at least one dance with her. At least one reel or country dance, for their friendship's sake. Indeed, it would seem odd if he did not invite her to the floor, given how long they had known one another.

Samuel kept pace with him, a wide grin stretching his features. "I cannot wait to see what has become of Miss Clark. She must have blossomed into a great beauty for you to be so smitten after a single meeting."

Robert stopped abruptly in the downstairs entry, and a

footman took the opportunity to approach and help him remove his hat and coat. "I am not smitten," he insisted. "Merely in a hurry to join the party. You know I cannot abide arriving late to an event of such importance."

"A lack of punctuality is to be blamed for your scowl?" Samuel asked with a chuckle, handing off his own outer things to another servant. He ran a gloved hand through his hair, tousling it somewhat. "You are not fooling me, Rob. I have not seen you this impatient about a ball in— well, never, come to think of it."

Grinding his teeth together, Robert turned away from his brother and took a deep breath in through the nose. If Samuel put the motivation behind Robert's actions on Penny's doorstep, others would as well. Maybe even Penny herself. That would amount to nothing more than his humiliation and disappointment.

"Perhaps I am excited to see Miss Clark," Robert said slowly, as though that made up for his earlier haste. "She is a friend I have not seen in ages. We did not have time to speak when we met on the road yesterday. I am eager to hear how she has passed the time since we parted seven years ago."

Samuel raised a skeptical eyebrow. "You are eager to chat with her, hm? To find out about her schooling, her come-out ball, perhaps even what books she has read of late?" Each word dripped with disbelief.

"Yes. Of course." Robert adjusted his waistcoat, then dropped his hands to his side. The nervous habit would out him as surely as anything. Admitting that he wished to see Penny again to satisfy his boyish affection for her would prove foolish. Especially as he was not in a position to do more than admire her from afar.

"Then we had better find her for this riveting conversation." Samuel put a hand on Robert's shoulder and pushed him toward the stairs and the first floor, where the ball took place. "I cannot wait to learn whether she prefers poetry to prose, the classics to the more modern authors, and if she has become an accomplished reader."

Pressing his lips together firmly, Robert allowed Samuel to push and prod him up the stairs and into the ballroom. Robert finally set his heels and shrugged off his brother's hand. Then he gave Samuel what he hoped was a quelling glare. "If you do something to embarrass Miss Clark—"

"I would never dream of humiliating a lady." Samuel smirked and started peering around the room. "*You*, on the other hand, would be great sport to tease. Especially since I have never seen you even act interested in a young lady, though there are many in town who are quite lovely."

"There are not many willing to wed a steward," Robert muttered, too quietly for Samuel to hear given his state of distraction.

Despite himself, Robert found his eyes searching for Penny, too. But while Samuel looked along the walls, Robert knew she would be dancing. Her loveliness would attract attention, the novelty of a new young lady would make her sought after, and if she smiled in the direction of any man, the gentleman would be helpless to do anything but ask to escort her to the floor.

As he suspected, Penny was dancing. He recognized her at once, and his breath caught at the beautiful sight she made in a dress the shade of rubies. The dress flowed over her curves, showing her figure to great advantage when she skipped lightly around the man partnering her for the reel. Yet while he admired her form, it was the bright smile upon her face which drew him forward. He had seen that smile a thousand times in their youth, whenever Penny had been particularly happy.

Many a time, he had been the cause of that joyful expression. That another man had done something to be awarded such a smile made Robert's heart ache.

Samuel rejoined Robert when he stopped at the very edge of the crowd watching the dance. From the corner of his eye, Robert saw Samuel study Miss Clark, then study Robert. A gleam of recognition appeared in his eyes.

"I can see why she captured your attention again, even after all these years. Miss Clark is quite pretty."

Pretty did not even begin to describe her. But rather than sound like a lovesick calf, Robert gave a brief nod. "She is, yes. But above that, Miss Clark is my friend. Or at least she used to be. I cannot think of a scrape or an adventure she did not take part in when we were home for the summer."

"Father did call her your little shadow." Samuel sounded thoughtful at the recollection. "I am afraid I did not take as much notice of her then. I spent most of my time with her brothers."

Robert withdrew before Penny noticed him standing there, he eased back into the crowd; Samuel followed. It would only confirm to Samuel that Robert was smitten if he stood and stared at Penny while she danced with another. He knew where she was and could approach her after the set. In the meantime, he ought to mingle with his neighbors.

Samuel kept near him for a short time, then took his

leave to speak to a friend he spied near the orchestra. Robert watched him go, engaged in his own conversation with Phillip Macon, the young Baron Heatherton. Phillip had nearly completed his studies at Oxford and had a mind to return to managing the holdings left to him by his late father, the countess's first husband.

"I know it would be wise to engage a steward. I cannot let the earl's steward continue to manage my affairs when I return home." The younger man sighed and gave Robert a narrow-eyed appraisal. "Do you think I could tempt you away from my cousin? I would trust your advice, Ellsworth."

At that moment, Harry Devon appeared at Robert's elbow. "Ah, I heard that. It is a very good thing I saw you both. How dare you, Phillip?" He snorted and leveled a glare at his cousin. "Ellsworth is quite content at White-wood. We have far too many projects for him to even consider abandoning me to look after things alone."

With a laugh, Robert crossed his arms and looked between the two men. Once, he had been their peer. Now, though they all laughed at Harry's act, Robert knew well enough he could not consider himself their equal. Harry Devon paid his salary, and Phillip Macon held a title. Both were above him in station.

"Though I admit that such an offer is flattering," he said to the baron, "I am content where I am, near my family's estate." He kept his ear on the music, noting the second dance in the set had begun. A brief glance in the direction of the couples was all he needed to find Penny's fine figure in that bright red dress, still promenading on the arm of another gentleman.

The cousins started speaking of their properties,

bemoaning the state of the weather and what it meant for their lands. The subject of the weather had been discussed by everyone for weeks, which made it an easy one to fall into. Robert joined the gentlemen in speculating when it might finally grow cold enough to freeze the mud and perhaps turn the rain to snow, but thus far no one held out hopes for such events until February. The old farmers all swore that was the earliest they could expect an end to the wretched mud and flooding.

Robert glanced to where Penny danced again, his eyes lingering on her when she laughed. Despite the music and the crowd, he heard the light sound and released his breath in a sigh.

"Do you know her?" Devon asked.

Robert snapped his attention back to the other two gentlemen, a confused denial upon his lips, when he realized Devon was asking his cousin the question.

"I met her only this evening," the baron said. "She is Miss Clark, a guest of Mr. and Mrs. Brody. Her uncle and aunt are her guardians."

"I must invite her to our Twelfth Night ball." Devon crossed his arms. "Daisy will extend the invitation, of course, but I imagine she would not mind. Will she be here through Epiphany, I wonder?"

Though he wished to stay silent on the matter, Robert cleared his throat before saying, "She will be here a fortnight, I believe. Miss Clark and I are well-acquainted, from childhood."

"That would make sense." Macon gave a brief nod. "She said her family leased that house near yours. What took her away, I wonder?"

"I remember now." Devon rocked back on his heels.

"She has two older brothers. Their parents died in a carriage accident, did they not? The bridge in Kettering."

Robert's heart dropped at the mention of the event that had separated him from Penny for the last seven years, leaving her an orphan. He had been at school when it happened, when he received word from his father of his dear friend's loss and subsequent removal from the county.

Everything in him had wished to fly to her aid, to find her, to hold her near and assure her he would look after her. His first instinct upon seeing her again had been to take her up in his arms and offer comfort, but it would be seven years too late, and completely inappropriate. Unwanted, even.

The baron made a sound of interest, but then turned the conversation to another topic entirely. All three of the men, Robert realized, had lost parents at an early age. The baron had lost his father, Devon his mother, and Robert his mother, too. Life was too fragile a thing, and death too quick to snatch away parents before their children had learned to manage on their own.

The music's tempo changed to indicate the set coming to an end. Robert murmured a quick excuse to Devon and the baron, then moved to the line of dancers just as they began clapping to thank the musicians for their efforts.

Robert took up a position behind Penny, but not too close, in hopes of catching her eye. To approach her would seem presumptuous, but if she saw him and did more than offer a nod of acknowledgement, he might ask her to dance. Had he been in a better position, had he the title of gentleman rather than steward, he would not hesitate to ask for a set outright.

She took the arm of her partner. Robert finally realized she had been dancing with Mr. Babcock, a gentleman with more orchards than sense. Yet he had a fine estate, and everyone knew him to be a genial fellow.

Penny saw Robert immediately, and her expression changed from one of pleasant enjoyment to true delight.

"Mr. Ellsworth, you came." Her escort immediately stopped, but Robert kept his eyes upon Penny. Her cheeks were rosy with her pleasure and exercise, her eyes bright, and a dimple in one cheek appeared with the width of her smile. He had not seen that dimple in more than seven years, yet knew at once he had missed it.

"Of course, Miss Clark. I could not pass up the opportunity to share a dance with one of my dearest friends." He bowed, then offered an apologetic smile to Mr. Babcock, who appeared to have wilted somewhat in the moments since the dance ended. "If you will excuse me, Mr. Babcock, I wish to ask this lady for a dance."

"You do mean a set, I hope," she corrected, releasing Mr. Babcock with only a polite nod before taking Robert's arm. Poor fellow seemed ready to cede defeat. Until Penny graced him with a gentler version of the smile she gave to Robert. "Thank you so much for an enjoyable quarter hour, Mr. Babcock. I have not had such a lovely time dancing for ages. I do hope I will see you again during my stay with the Brodys."

Mr. Babcock lit up again as she spoke, bowed, and promised to call upon her soon. Then he left, chest puffed out and a knowing smirk cast in Robert's direction.

"Now you have done it," Robert said, voice lowered.

Penny looked up at him, her eyebrows raised. "What have I done, precisely?"

"Encouraged Mr. Babcock." Robert shook his head and affected a tragic frown. "He will beset you with hothouse flowers and calling cards for the remainder of your stay."

Penny laughed, though not unkindly. "That would be most attentive of him. I cannot say many gentlemen have gone to such lengths for me before. His interest will wane before my visit is through, I am certain."

Robert took her to the foot of the couples lining up for the next set of dances. "You cannot be serious." He released her to her place in the line and had to take in a deep breath when her loveliness hit him squarely in the heart a second time. "You must be regularly flooded with gifts from admirers."

Her smile notably faded away, and she dropped her eyes to the floor between them a moment. "Not so, Mr. Ellsworth."

He hated to see her sad, to see the light in her eyes dim. Especially due to something he had said. Instead of allowing her to remain with eyes downcast, Robert searched his memory for something to speak upon that would take her back to a happier time. "Do you remember," he said, somewhat abruptly, "when you hid in the hay after harvest?"

With a wrinkle above her nose and with lowered lashes, she responded without hesitation. "How could I forget? I thought it such a clever hiding place until I spent the rest of the week with my arms and legs itching as though a thousand fleas had claimed me as their host. Who would have thought there was a nettle mixed in with that particular pile of straw?"

The woman to Penny's right gasped and shot them a dark look, which caused Penny to blush. "Oh, I beg your pardon." Fleas were not, apparently, a topic permitted while dancing. Yet Penny started to smile at him as they took the opportunity to join hands and execute a series of steps and turns before stopping in place, higher up the row than before.

"What brought that memory to your mind?" she asked when they settled to stare at one another again, waiting for their turn in the dance.

Though he could not admit his real purpose, Robert had another answer readily at hand. "I am fairly certain that I was the one littering your entry with my offers of consolation in those days. So, you cannot say you have never had such attentions."

She glowered at him, though a smile still tugged at her lips. "You were fourteen, Mr. Robert Ellsworth. I am not certain that counts as a gentleman giving a lady his attention."

They both laughed, then took up the dance again, looping around each other with barely more than a brush of their fingers, then back away again, bowing to the partners on either side of them and waiting once more to move up to the head of the dancing couples.

He had missed her. Missed her laughter, her jests, the way her lips curled upward slowly just before she allowed herself to give in to her humor. The girl he had known was there, but she had changed, too.

Almost as though she had followed the trail of his thought, Penny said, "You have grown so much taller. It is not at all fair that I have stayed precisely the same height since I was fifteen."

Without a care for where they were, Robert hunched his shoulders and dropped his head forward, chin on his chest. "Is that better? I should not wish you to feel too short."

She laughed and swatted his arm before taking it as the dance called for, then turned and walked around another couple. They were nearly halfway down the row at this point, the dance itself half over. He hated that. If only he could stay dancing with her all evening.

"I quite prefer your new height, thank you." She tipped her head to one side, a chestnut curl falling artfully to brush against her bare neck as she did. The look she gave him was almost flirtatious, which made his heart perform acrobatics it had no business even practicing.

Robert needed to change the subject, needed to stop flirting. Nothing could come of it. Entering into a flirtation with Penny wouldn't be a friendly thing to do, but selfish, and it would only hurt when she left at the end of Twelfth Night. "My height does come in handy on occasion," he quipped, trying to sound more indifferent and less teasing.

"I imagine you can reach all the highest shelves in the library and the best plums in the trees." She tossed him a saucy look over her shoulder when she bowed to the gentleman at his right, then looped around the woman to hers. In another few moments, they faced each other again. The dance kept them moving, but it hardly interrupted their conversation. There were too many couples performing each movement.

"I can also reach the shelf where the apothecary keeps the sweets," he admitted, somewhat gruffly, watching as her hips swayed just a touch with her movement. He snatched his eyes back. Only a cad would notice such a thing, he was certain, especially in a best friend. How could he get back on an even footing with her? Teasing had swiftly led to flirting, and he could not do that.

Friendship was the order of the evening. Perhaps he ought not dance the rest of the set with her. He needed to clear his head. To make sense of where he had gone wrong.

"I wish it were not such dreadful weather," she said, forcing him back to the conversation. "I should like to go exploring all our old haunts, but I imagine most are mired in mud and are not fit to be seen at present. If the pond would freeze over as it did when we were younger, we could go skating."

The childish games of the past were a safe topic, even if the way she regarded him made his heart stutter. "Skating, building villages of snow people, and running home to hot cider after. Those were the best days, were they not?"

"They were. Then you always had to go and ruin things by returning to school." She gave him a look of mock disapproval. "I missed you so when you left at the end of every holiday."

They were veering into dangerous territory again. Robert cleared his throat. He would not admit how much he disliked leaving her behind, and he certainly would not tell her how much he had missed her when he returned home, knowing she would never be there to greet him again. The loss of her parents had to have devastated her. The loss of her company had left him in mourning for quite some time.

"How have you kept yourself entertained these last several years without me?" The slight flirtation in his question surprised him. Had she sensed the hopefulness in how he spoke to her? Robert *needed* to steer the conversation another direction, *needed* her to speak of the same details she would share with a near stranger. Yet he *wanted* to ask after her thoughts, her dreams, and her heart. He cleared his throat. "I am sure you managed perfectly well, of course."

If she did not think him a bumbling fool by the end of the evening, he would be grateful.

CHAPTER 6

Men were entirely too confusing. One moment Robert jested with her, the next he pulled back as though they barely knew one another. Though many years had passed, the moment Penny laid eyes upon him she knew what mattered most, their connection and friendship, had not changed. She had worried their second meeting would be as strange as the first but knew now she had only taken him by surprise the day before. Having anticipated seeing him all day long, and hoping he did the same, made it that much easier to converse as though the intervening years had never been.

Except that Robert kept dancing about in the conversation as he was in the figures required for the country dance.

"I have done as most young ladies. I entered a new school for a short time, then kept my aunt company. I write my brothers long letters; they hardly write at all." Penny shifted from one foot to the other, taking in Robert's easy posture and the slant of his shoulders with approval. He had grown into an attractive man, which made a great deal of sense as he had been an attractive boy. Not that she had ever told him such a thing. "I understand you have had a great deal to busy yourself as well. Your education and now your new position."

Robert's shoulders drooped and his expression tightened. "Ah. You have heard about that." He did not sound especially enthusiastic to discuss his work. "Mr. Devon needed assistance. I am fortunate I was nearby when he expressed his thoughts on the matter. It was actually his wife, formerly Miss Ames, who suggested we might suit each other."

That made Penny laugh. "I remember Daisy Ames quite well. She would be sensible enough to suggest such an arrangement. Isn't it interesting how the two of them are now wed? You never quite expect matches like that, between people you know." Indeed, she had learned that many of her childhood friends had wed the very same boys who were friends with her brothers and with Robert.

He had gone all stiff again with the turn in their conversation. Did speaking of the Devons make him uncomfortable, as they were his employers? Or was it marriage he objected to? With no wish to make him miserable, Penny changed subjects again, babbling on about her brothers. She did not speak about Frederick long, for he was soon to wed, but she could mention Daniel's place in the army with ease.

Slowly, Robert relaxed, and even asked questions. He did not tease her again. Perhaps she had been too forward. Just because she felt as though nothing between them had changed did not mean he felt the same. The only topics she would discuss would be those permitted among the most proper and polite of society.

This meant the conversation grew duller with each passing moment, and they finished the first dance at the head of the line. The musicians paused, accepting the applause as their due. Robert shifted around to look at her, and Penny realized with a start that he had never accepted, never actually asked, for more than the one dance. It had been she who presumptuously said he must mean a set instead of a single dance.

The right thing to do would be to allow him to escape, if he wished. Perhaps there was another young lady he wished to spend his evening with. What if he had only sought out Penny due to the obligation of their former friendship? Heart stricken at the thought, Penny spoke without as much grace as she had meant.

"That was my fifth dance this evening. As we are very old friends, would you mind terribly if I used this time to get some refreshment? Perhaps I need some fresh air as well." She looked in the direction of the tall windows and the doors leading out to a balcony and the gardens. If he abandoned her, she would know at once she had misunderstood the appreciative look in his eyes when she accepted his offer of a dance. She would see that she had been away too long, that she meant nothing to him.

His expression faltered, looking disappointed rather than relieved. At least, that was what she thought the downturn of his lips communicated, the fall of his shoulders bespeaking defeat rather than relaxation.

"Of course," he said, tone softer then before. "If that is what you wish. Would you like me to return you to your aunt, or fetch you a lemonade? Cider, perhaps?" His gaze searched hers, darting across her face.

Tamping down her own relief, Penny offered him a small smile. They had moved away from the dancing, standing beneath the landing where the chaperones and matrons stood above the din conversing. "That is kind of you. Perhaps we—"

"Robert." A stern male voice broke through her words, startling her. They both turned to see a man who appeared strikingly similar to Robert, though broader in shoulder and somewhat less attractive in Penny's opinion, standing no more than three feet from them. "Do the right thing, or shall swoop in and accomplish the matter for you?" Then Samuel—for who else could it be?—looked pointedly upward.

Penny's eyes darted up, along with Robert's, and her lips parted in surprise. A kissing ball. She had forgotten all about them, had not given them another thought once she had spotted Robert; the fear of being caught beneath one with a stranger had disappeared in her delight of being with her dearest of friends.

When her eyes fell again to meet Robert's gaze, she could not name the myriad of emotions flashing in his eyes, but she easily recognized the embarrassment coloring his cheeks and ears. Was she too plain to even kiss? Her heart fell clear to her stomach, and she went cold all over.

"Robert," she murmured, "you do not have to if you do not want to." Someone else, a gentleman she thought she recognized, appeared near Samuel's shoulder, a woman on his arm.

"Ah, has that kissing ball caught another couple?" He

nodded to the woman on his arm. "I confess, my wife and I had a similar difficulty but moments ago." He raised his eyebrows suggestively and grinned. "Only one thing for it, old man."

The woman tossed her head and laughed; the sound was not unkind, yet it did all the more damage to Penny's fragile heart. "Do not mind him, miss. What he does not know is that I tricked him beneath the mistletoe myself."

Did Robert think she had done that to him? Tricked him? Penny met his eyes again, frantically trying to communicate to him she had not even noticed the kissing ball. Oh, if he had a young lady to please somewhere in the crowd, would this make her angry? If Robert was Penny's suitor, she would not like to learn of him kissing anyone else, kissing ball or not.

The embarrassment had disappeared from his features and, in its place, a look of determination met her. His eyes darkened, staring at her with an intensity she did not understand. Did he mean to reject her, then? But then he bent forward, and just before his lips touched hers whispered three words for her ears only. "I am sorry." Then he kissed her, and everything within her warmed with pleasure even though tears sprang to her eyes.

Sorry? She had dreamed of this kiss since she was fifteen years old and realized she had fallen in love with her best friend. Except this was not how it was supposed to happen. And Robert, in her dreams, had been as eager as she to experience the blissful moment of their first kiss.

Warmth curled in her stomach, despite her aching heart. The kiss lasted no more than a few seconds. Long enough that no one could tease Robert over a peck, but quick enough none could mistake it for more than what it had been—an obligation.

Penny stepped back as soon as Robert's lips left hers, curling her hands into fists. She tried to laugh, but the sound came out somewhat strangled. She could not look at him. Would not meet his eyes. Instead, she looked directly at Samuel.

"There, now you will have to try your luck with some other lady, sir." She curtsied. "Always good to see you, Mr. Ellsworth." Though she looked at Samuel, she swiftly took her leave of Robert.

As she dashed away, making directly for her aunt spied in the corner, a tear slipped from her eye. She brushed it away with one gloved finger and pasted on a smile to rival the chandeliers in its brightness. Penny had no intention of communicating her feelings to the whole room.

In a single moment, a lifelong friendship had been ruined. How could she face Robert again, knowing how much he had disliked even the idea of kissing her beneath the mistletoe?

CHAPTER 7

R obert could have kissed Penny a thousand times over and never grown weary of it. Of that he was certain from the instant their lips touched to when they parted. With his brother and the ridiculous couple looking on, Robert had to keep his feet planted firmly in reality, however.

Though Penny had disappeared too quickly for Robert to take hold of his senses and follow, he did not forget to reach up and claim one of the silver berries from the kissing ball. Then he had grabbed Samuel by the arm and dragged him into a corner to give his brother a severe dressing-down.

With the berry tucked in his waistcoat pocket, Robert left the ball. He had no wish to see the hurt in Penny's eyes again, nor try to spend the whole night avoiding her. One ridiculous tradition had somehow ruined everything between them. All he had wanted, all he had hoped for, was an invitation to see her again before she left Annes-bury and Kettering for wherever her aunt and uncle called home. He wanted time with her, to enjoy her presence, possibly to put some dreams away at last merely by saying a proper goodbye.

Yet the ball had been a disaster, and the one sweet moment of the evening when he had been permitted to at long last kiss the girl he had admired for so long, was bittersweet. That kiss had been the moment to ruin the ball for Penny. For him.

The next morning, Robert instructed the footman assisting him during his stay to pack his things as he would return to his own home that evening.

When he came down to breakfast, Peter was already present, the crumbs of his pastry hopefully not settling on the pages of the book he read at the table. "Robert, how was the ball?" his younger brother asked after a hasty swallow.

Robert scowled and loaded a plate from the sideboard. "Tolerable."

"Then I am justified in my decision not to attend," Peter said smartly, turning back to his book. "Every ball is nothing more than an extension of the marriage mart, and I'm too young to be leg-shackled."

"Who is getting shackles?" Samuel asked, entering the room and having the audacity to walk about with a swagger.

Dropping his plate on the table with more of a clatter than he intended, Robert winced as he groused. "No one." Certainly not him. Not ever him. Who would deign him a suitable match? Perhaps a wealthy farmer's daughter. A merchant's daughter, even, if her father were not too successful. No one at that ball.

"Are you still grumbling about the kissing incident?"

Samuel turned from the sideboard, a spoon full of preserves still in his hand. "It was a kiss, Rob. Not a proposal."

Peter's book closed with a snap. "What is all this about kissing?"

"The room was littered with kissing balls," Samuel informed their younger brother, a crooked smile on his face. "Robert had the misfortune, or so he views it, of standing directly beneath one such piece of greenery. With Miss Clark."

A low whistle escaped Peter's mouth, causing both his brothers to glare at him. Peter glanced from one to the other. "Are we not permitted to whistle in this house?"

"Not at the table," Samuel and Robert chorused together, and that finally broke through Robert's sullen mood. He chuckled and added, "Mother never allowed it, so Father did not either."

"'Good manners prohibit us making sounds like animals at the table,'" Samuel said, quoting their mother directly. She had passed ten years previous. "No whistling, grunting, growling, chirping, snorting, or howling." He chuckled and leaned back in his chair.

"I withdraw my whistle then." Peter put his book on the table and folded his arms as he leaned back. "But do tell me about this incident with Miss Clark. Robert kissed her?"

"Indeed. Which, given our previous conversation you might remember from yesterday, I was given to believe he would find the moment enjoyable. Instead, Robert faced down Miss Clark as though he had been asked to kiss a hedgehog."

"No." Peter shifted to lean across the table toward Robert. "You were reluctant to kiss her?"

"A gentleman does not discuss such things," Robert muttered, stabbing at a piece of ham. Of course, his brothers would not let the subject go that easily.

"Reluctant does not begin to describe it. The man had the very expression of the condemned going to the gallows." Samuel buttered his toast with sudden strokes of the knife. "And she, poor woman, took the kiss in the same form. You have never seen a woman so disappointed—"

"That does not speak well of your technique, Robert." Peter laughed.

Robert's appetite fled. He dropped his face in his hands and rested his elbows upon the table. Discussing his thoughts and feelings regarding Penny would be foolish. Samuel, only suspecting Robert harbored more than friendship in his heart, had already made a mess of things, and Peter would be no help at all. "Can we leave off discussing Miss Clark, if you please? I would like to eat my breakfast in peace, and then it is Boxing Day. There are other things for us to accomplish."

"Gifts for the servants," Samuel said with a nod. "And a box to the church. I know. Everything is prepared. There are envelopes with every servant's name and the appropriate amount in them."

"They have put up with a lot from you the past year," Robert reminded Samuel, leaping upon the new topic almost desperately. Household matters were a far safer thing to discuss than Penny.

The conversation remained on the arrangements for

the distribution of the envelopes with extra funds, a gift to each servant, and the poor boxes were full of articles of clothing and baskets for charitable distribution. After their mother passed, with no woman of the house to see to such things, their father had involved each of the boys in the kind work. He had instilled in them a spirit of gratitude from a young age, and from that the obligation to assist those less fortunate than themselves.

Never mind that when he passed away their estate had nearly collapsed. Samuel still wrestled with the financial aspects, or rather, the debts their father left behind. In his last years, he had made many poor decisions his sons still worked to correct. Samuel, by living frugally and seeking advice from other landowners, and Robert by working for Mr. Devon. Peter's education was also something Robert paid for from his own pocket. He did not want his brother to end up working for another man if he could be independent in his pursuits.

Two hours after breakfast, the brothers mounted their horses and followed the dogcart, stacked high with provisions and gifts for the poor in the community, to the church.

"At least it is not raining yet today," Peter said, eyeing the gray skies with a puckered brow. "I cannot think much more of this is good for us."

"It isn't," Robert said, his eyes on the land surrounding them. "All the best soil will be washed away. Tenants will have leaky roofs and ill children. The wood stores will grow rot. We need at least a few weeks to recover, but I worry we will not get it."

"How is Devon fairing during this confounded flooding?" Samuel asked, keeping his eye on the horse and cart plodding along before them. "I have ordered several repairs to our three cottagers' buildings, but I imagine there will be more necessary soon."

"Building the new cottages last winter has kept us from needing to make repairs." Robert adjusted his hold on the reins and nudged his horse to avoid a particularly nasty hole in the road, filled to the brim with muddy water. "His land is higher than most, too. The loss of good soil is the biggest worry and keeping the sheep healthy."

"While I am relieved you both worry over the practical matters," Peter said from behind them, his youthful energy giving a bounce to his words, "I am more concerned with what the rain will do to the rest of the festivities. People will not go out to celebrate and there will be fewer parties and fun if we are all sitting beside our fires to stay warm and dry."

Samuel chuckled. "You make it sound like we're in our dotage, with aching bones."

"Robert is in his dotage." Peter rode his horse between them, forcing Robert to pull more to the side. "He cannot even kiss a girl without mustering up the will to do so."

"Not this again." Robert glared over Peter's head at Samuel, who was doing a rather poor job at pretending disinterest. "Samuel has given you the wrong idea about that kiss, and about Miss Clark."

"And about your feelings for Miss Clark?" Samuel asked, his tone one of feigned innocence.

"Yes. You are especially wrong about that." Robert spied the church's tower with its bell. At least the inquisition would be over soon. Might as well try to assuage his brothers' curiosity. "I have missed her friendship. I was closer to no one else, not even the two of you, before Miss

Clark and her brothers had to leave to live with their relations. We had always been good friends. Meeting again, after so much time has passed, made it difficult to know which foot to stand on with her. I had nearly sorted it out when Samuel insisted, rather like an ill-mannered theater-goer, that I kiss her beneath the kissing ball."

Peter whistled, and Robert glared at him. He saw Samuel do the same.

"Am I not to whistle out of doors, either?" he asked, somewhat incredulously.

Ignoring Peter, Samuel pointed directly at Robert. "You wanted to kiss her. Admit it, and then I swear I will not bring it up again."

"I make no such promises."

Peter grinned and his horse pushed forward, going around the cart to arrive at the church just before them.

"I will admit nothing." Robert followed Peter, though with greater restraint.

Samuel dismounted moments after Robert and immediately clapped him on the back. "I do not know why you fight it. She is a lovely woman. You two have a great deal of history together. Why not pursue her, Rob? At least to see what happens?"

Admitting why to Samuel would give rise to an argument between them, regarding finances and marriage, and who knew what else. Though Samuel might return the estate to prosperity, it would not help Robert's situation. He would still not be a man of property. He lived in a house given to him by his employer, after all.

They entered the church without Robert's answer, the pews stacked with baskets and boxes of every size already and many women milling about making notes on slates while gentlemen stood along the walls conversing with one another. Mr. Ames and his curate, Mr. Haskett, were near the front of the building and conversing with Lady Annesbury.

Before Robert saw Penny, he knew she was within the church. There was a humming in his ears, a warmth at his side, and then the most delicious smell of cinnamon, just before a hand touched his forearm.

"Penny." He spoke her name the instant before he looked down, meeting her steady gaze. "I did not know you would be here." She winced. Had it sounded as though he did not like finding her present? He hastily added, "Most do not come after the late evening at the ball."

At that, her cheeks turned pink. Of course. He had reminded her of the kiss. Robert opened his mouth to apologize again, to explain, though he knew not what more he might say on the matter, when the hand on his arm fluttered away.

"Please, Robert. Let us not discuss what happened at the ball. Ever. We will pretend it did not happen and resume our friendship as before." She spoke with such firmness, despite her low turn, that he could do nothing more than swallow his words and nod. She looked out the door. "Have you many baskets to bring inside?"

"Yes. We were not certain where to put them."

She lifted a slate and chalk. "It might be best to leave them in a cart. I can inventory what you have brought. We may already know where to send your goods." She took a step to the door, and he joined her. Never mind that Samuel ought to be the one to see to the duty. Samuel had done enough damage already and could not be counted on to keep his mouth shut upon the matter of Robert's feelings. If the eldest Ellsworth said a word to Penny on his suspicions regarding Robert, all hope for any acquaintance and comfortable farewell would be lost.

Worst of all, he feared his heart would be lost, too.

CHAPTER 8

Though Penny had spent most of the previous evening thinking over Robert's kiss, she had no wish to discuss it with him. Given his great reluctance to kiss her in the first place, it was the safest course for her to take. Even approaching him had been difficult. Then, touching him had elicited an excitable sensation, like that of electric currents, running through her from her fingertips to her toes. She had to forget the kiss.

Having him at her heels while she walked around the dogcart, writing out what he and his brothers had brought to give to the poor, did little to steady her nerves. Yet Penny kept her chin up. She had been praised for her acting abilities in school when the girls put on plays for one another's amusement. Managing to pretend herself above the giddiness inspired by Robert's nearness would not prove too difficult. She hoped, at least.

"How is it," Robert asked from only a few inches behind her, "that a guest of our parish is out in the cold doing this work?" When she cast him a perplexed look over her shoulder, he ducked his head slightly. "Not even those who live here offer any help to the poor."

"This used to be one of my favorite parts of all the celebrations," Penny answered honestly, averting her eyes from his. "My mother saw to it that I came with her, every year, to help dress the baskets in ribbons. I put ginger-bread cookies shaped like stars in every basket, whether they went to homes with children or not."

"Gingerbread cookies were always your favorite."

She cast him a quick glance, surprised he remembered. "They still are."

A slow, hesitant smile appeared on his face. "I remember now, how you used to scurry from basket to basket. Father never let us stay in the church long. We brought our things, then he set us on our way. He said it was always better for the women to deliver the goods. People are more likely to accept help when offered in gentleness."

"Perhaps." She made a final notation. "Five quilts. How did a household of three gentlemen come up with so many?"

"Oh, those are compliments of my housekeeper. She sews and gives the blankets away. She has no family and sent them with me today." He reached into the basket with the quilts and lifted one out enough so its pattern could be seen. "She uses all the scrap material from the house, so they are rather varied, but I suppose one might still call them pretty."

He had a housekeeper? That spoke well of his position with the Devons. Penny stood on her toes the better to peer at the quilt. There were deep browns and reds, some greens, all in simple blocks and triangles sewn together.

"It is quite beautiful. The practical colors will likely be appreciated by many, too."

She lowered herself back to the ground. "Thank you, Robert. This is a lovely contribution. I will see to it Lady Annesbury and Mr. Ames are informed."

That tentative look came into his eyes again, as though he were afraid of what she might say next, what she might do. As there were no kissing balls about, she did not think he had much to fear from her. She nearly said so, but instead cleared her throat and looked away.

"Will you go to the Twelfth Night masque?" Robert blurted, startling her into looking at him again.

"The Devon masque? I believe Mrs. Boyd mentioned it. I think we might. Does Mrs. Devon send out assignments before such events, or do we discover our part to play upon arrival?" she asked.

He had tucked his hands behind his back and lowered his head, looking up at her through his eyelashes. "I am not certain. It is the first year she has hosted a ball for Twelfth Night. I understand she wishes for the members of the community to have all the enjoyment of a masque ball without worrying about the somewhat immoral connotations with such a fete."

"If I could be any character at a masque," Penny went on to say, hoping to find the old familiarity of their conversation through her rambling, "I should like to be a Greek muse, or the personification of a virtue. Those should be easier than a more outlandish character. I went to a masque two years previous where everyone was to be a character from English history. There was even a Caesar who went about with his nose in the air, attempting to tell everyone else what to do." She lowered her voice and leaned a touch closer to Robert than was strictly necessary. "I was invited at the last possible moment, so my part was hardly interesting. They made me Hilda of Whitby, and I confess to not remembering that woman at all."

Robert's interest returned, with a slight spark in his brown eyes. He leaned a little closer. She ignored the way her heart danced at his nearness. "What did you do, not knowing who you played?"

"I acted only as myself, I am afraid, until someone took pity upon me and said I was a Saint from the Dark Ages. The patron saint of poetry." She laughed and lowered her slate. "I went about quoting scripture and poetry alike the rest of the evening. It was such fun." Offering her his arm, Robert escorted her back into the warmth of the church. "I am glad to hear you made the most of it. I am a terrible actor."

"You ought to request an easy role for yourself at the masque," she put in brightly.

At that comment, Robert's look changed to one a little more serious. "Perhaps I shall. Though it should be more entertaining, I think, if I had a costume to match another."

They had stopped just inside the church door, near the last pew. Others still moved about inside, organizing, talking in low voices.

"Like the king and queen of hearts," she suggested, "or Romeo and Juliet." Realizing she had suggested costumes fit for a romantic couple, Penny met his curious gaze with a merry smile. Let him think she teased him. That would be better than admitting she imagined herself in the role to match his. "I suppose you should have to have a young lady to take on the role of your opposite for such a thing.

Have you such a woman who would be willing to do so?" Then she bit her tongue, smiling through the pain.

At least acting like a ninny might help her find out, at last, if there was a woman in Robert's life he had yet to mention.

He hesitated overlong, his eyes going to the front of the church where the windows let in what little sunlight was to be had. "If I am to be honest, there is a woman I should wish to fill such a role." He heaved a sigh at the same moment her heart cracked. Then he squared his shoulders, as though making up his mind, and gave her a broad smile. "But she hasn't any idea that I think of her with such fondness, so such a costume is unlikely in my future."

"Oh, Robert." Despite her disappointment, the pricking of her heart, knowing his heart was in a similar state gave her pain. "You should make her aware of your feelings. You might be surprised—"

He cut her off with a sharp shake of his head, releasing her arm. "She is far above my reach, I think. But let us not worry over it." Robert took a step back, putting enough distance between them she no longer felt the warmth of his body. "I must take my leave. I am expected back at the Devon house. Whitewood. They have their own Boxing Day traditions I am to take part in."

"Oh. You are back to your work, then?" Her shoulders fell. "My aunt and I intended to visit tomorrow. Visit your family home. I am determined to show her all the places I spent my childhood." Penny had hoped Robert might still be there, might even act as a guide, but that was silly of her. The man had other responsibilities. He could not see to her every whim merely because she was on holiday.

"Samuel will be delighted to host you, I am certain." Nothing in the run of Robert's lips indicated his disappointment; if anything he appeared happy again. Happy for her. The cheerful countenance made her heart ache all the more, knowing he concealed feelings for a woman who likely had no idea that a man as honorable and kind as Robert loved her.

Penny nodded her acceptance of his words, then looked down at the slate in her hands. "Well. I had better present this information to the countess." She stepped away, but Robert's hand landed gently upon her forearm. She stopped and looked back at him over her shoulder, her heart rising most unreasonably.

"I am glad you are here, Penny. I have missed you." He offered the words of friendship with a lowered voice and earnest expression, then released her and walked away without another word of farewell or anything else.

Without giving herself time to think on what those few words had done to her, Penny took up her responsibilities again, approaching the countess. Perhaps if she kept busy enough, she could avoid thinking about Robert altogether. At least until she found herself in a quiet moment, when she knew she would have to give her heart a stern lecture about harboring feelings of more than friendship for the generous boy who had grown into a most attractive and kind man.

CHAPTER 9

Robert sorted through yet another list of maintenance requests for the Devon house in Town, most of them related to the attics. The unusually wet winter had exposed every weakness in the house's roof, from leaks to lose shingling. The estate could afford the repairs, of course, but finding reputable craftsmen in London while he resided in the country would prove difficult. He could not go to London himself for some weeks but leaving the requests unanswered would prove only to worsen the state of things.

Burying himself in the work, writing out proposed budgets and how to go about finding men with the experience necessary to complete repairs, Robert nearly pushed his personal problems from his mind. Yet every time he paused in a calculation, Robert's thoughts went to Penny, standing in the misty morning light, eyes upon him, so close he wanted nothing more than to touch her.

Their kiss had plagued him, too. Visiting him in every quiet moment, reminding him of its lingering sweetness, and how she had run away after he pressed her lips with his.

Groaning, Robert dropped his pen on the blotter and pushed away from the desk. He started pacing, from his window to the door which separated his office from Devon's study. At times when the two men worked together, the door between them was open. Today it was closed, Mr. Devon being elsewhere in the house which suited Robert perfectly. He could pace the length of the room without worry over drawing Devon's notice.

He had no desire to explain himself and his agitated state to anyone else. "Hinting that I had feelings for her was foolish," Robert muttered to himself when he drew up to the window. Had he seemed desperate? She had not seemed to realize he spoke of her. A blessing, really, given how he had blurted out his feelings without thought. His brothers had obviously addled him with their conversation on the way to the church.

A knock on the door pulled him from his self-pitying thoughts. He adjusted his posture and called, "Come in."

The door opened, and Harry Devon strode inside, a good cheer evident in the wide smile upon his face. "Ellsworth, I am glad I caught you. I was not sure, given the lateness of the hour."

"Lateness—?" Robert pulled his timepiece from his pocket. After five o'clock. "I am afraid I did not notice. It has been so dark outside all day, it is difficult to keep track of the passing hours."

Devon came forward and leaned against the window, looking out into the darkness while the rain pattered against the glass. "Indeed. But this is perfect. Would you be willing to eat your evening meal here, with us? My wife has invited a visitor to stay to dinner, given the weather. We did not think it fair to send Miss Clark home. Given your prior history, I think it would make the evening more enjoyable."

Robert stood still as a marble statue, staring at his employer as though Devon had lost his mind. He had no intention of seeing Penny again so soon. The day before, stumbling over his words and their meanings in the church, he had been grateful for a reprieve. Surely, a few days apart from her would give him time to reorder his thoughts, collect himself, root himself firmly in friendship and nothing more.

A dinner party consisting of him, Penny, and the Devons could not come at a worse moment.

Yet he swallowed away all his protests and forced a genial smile. "I would be delighted. Thank you for the invitation."

"If the rain does not cease," Mr. Devon put in, tapping the glass with a finger, "I will need to escort Miss Clark and her maid home."

"No," Robert said firmly. "That will not do, sir."

Devon shifted, then tilted his head forward. "I am listening, Ellsworth. Why will it not do?"

Though Devon treated him as an equal, Robert never forgot he was on the man's payroll. They might be of an age, been raised with similar standards and financial backing, but circumstances changed. Devon could now buy up the services of a dozen men like Robert. They both knew it, even if Mr. Devon wanted to ignore it. Robert rarely found reason to correct or redirect his employer, but in this instance, he had to speak up.

"Miss Clark's parents died on a night like this, in a

carriage accident. While I cannot speak with certainty upon the state of her mind regarding that night, I cannot imagine riding out in similar circumstances would be an easy thing for her. Perhaps I overstep myself, but as it is for the sake of a lady's comfort, I hope you will forgive me when I suggest Mrs. Devon ought to invite her to stay the night instead."

"Of course, Ellsworth." Devon reached out and put a hand on Robert's shoulder. "I appreciate your insight in this matter. Indeed, in all matters. You have not yet given advice I found lacking." He stepped back, removing his hand, and tilted his head toward the door. "Shall we go to the ladies? Dinner tonight will be intimate. Daisy has decided we will not dress, as neither of our guests have the opportunity to do so."

"Your wife has ever been a sensible woman," Robert said, the tension in his shoulders easing somewhat. He put out the candles on his desk, then followed his employer out of the room. Mr. and Mrs. Devon fit together like a pair of gloves. Complimentary, a matched set, despite being near opposites at times in their ideas.

Robert walked through the long halls of the house, passing servants along the way as they lit sconces in the walls. Devon had mentioned the idea of having the house fitted for gas lights, but the undertaking would be expensive unless he could convince the entire community to switch to that form of lighting. It would be some time before Annesbury caught up with London and the larger cities of Britain.

They came to the doors of the parlor, where the Devons sat together until dinner was served, and Mr. Devon walked inside without so much as knocking.

Robert followed, hands tucked behind him. He bowed before he looked up, immediately catching Penny's eye. She watched him, a blush in her cheeks. She lowered her eyes to her lap where she fussed with the gloves she wore.

"I have prevailed upon Mr. Ellsworth, and he has graciously agreed to take his dinner with us." Devon grinned at Robert, then reached for his wife's hands. "Might you join me for a moment in the hall, love? I have a matter over which I would like your counsel. If you will excuse us, Miss Clark? Mr. Ellsworth?"

"Of course," Penny said easily, her light voice setting Robert's heart to beat a faster tempo than before.

"I will do my best to keep your guest company, Mrs. Devon," Robert promised, bowing again.

"I know you will." Mrs. Devon drifted through the room with her usual grace, her chin held up and a smile for her husband that felt almost too intimate for Robert to look upon. He averted his eyes to the floor, pressing his lips together to hide his own smirk. The Devons had started their courtship somewhat strangely, but he could not think of many couples he had seen who were happier in their choice of a spouse. They obviously loved each other.

He stepped closer to Penny and gestured to the seat beside her on the couch. "May I?"

"Please." She slid over a few inches, giving him more room than necessary. She wore a dress of deep blue, which contrasted beautifully with the pink in her cheeks. "I am glad you are here to join us. I cannot tell you how much I look forward to a better opportunity to speak with you." The words spilled from her as water cascaded from a fountain, clear and sweet, but rushed. "I went to your family's estate this morning, as my aunt and I planned. The weather kept our tour mostly indoors, but Samuel was very good to show us about. It seemed everywhere I turned I could see the ghosts of our childhood selves, playing and inventing all sorts of trouble." She took a breath, the color in her cheeks deepened and she lowered her eyes again. "We had a great many lovely days in that house, did we not?"

"We did." He shifted in his seat and ran his hand across the arm of the couch. He looked away from her, though studying her profile brought him every kind of happiness. "We were troublesome little creatures at times, if I remember correctly."

He saw her turn to him from the corner of his eye. "You always took the brunt of our punishment when we stepped too far across your father's line."

With a shrug, Robert shifted just enough to meet her gaze. "As was my duty, as a gentleman." He tilted his chin upward, trying to affect a noble expression. "What knight would ever allow a lady to suffer when he could prevent it? Besides." He lowered his voice and tipped toward her a few inches. "I think my father knew well enough you were equally to blame, but he liked you better than he liked me."

A light laugh escaped her, but not for more than a moment. What a moment that was. Penny shook her head and folded her hands primly in her lap. "Of course he liked me best. I am a lovely person. Everyone says so."

"Do they?" he teased. "I seem to recall a certain girl people thought 'lovely' pushing me into the lake. Pelting me with snowballs. Hiding frogs in my boots." He faced her more directly, holding up fingers for every misdeed he recounted. "Sneaking a mouse into my bedroom, and then a cat to catch it. That was a horrid night. Then there was the time—"

"Oh, do stop. You make me sound beastly." Her shoulders shook with laughter though she pressed her lips closed with her fingers, a likely effort to regain control of her amusement. Then she shook her finger at him. "You were just as terrible, you know. I pushed you into the lake because you insulted my bonnet."

"Those gray feathers made it appear as though a pigeon had nested upon it," he said with a casual shrug.

"And you threw snowballs right back. The frogs were merited, of course, because you threatened to leave them in my slippers. Then you—"

He caught her wrist to keep her finger from shaking in his direction. "I know. I made you think I put a mouse in your new reticule, which you then threw, and it landed in the mud. Yes. I remember. It was quite thoughtful of you to find a barn cat capable of hunting the beast down again. Though I have often wondered how you caught the mouse in the first place, when you were so frightened of them."

She raised her eyebrows. "I will never reveal that secret, in case I have need of using it again."

He laughed and his thumb idly slid across her wrist in an almost-caress. She sobered at his touch, her breathing stilled.

"It is decided," Mrs. Devon stated as she and her husband swept into the room. Robert hastily released Penny and moved as far as he could to the opposite end of the couch while she did the same. "Miss Clark will stay the night."

"Oh, how thoughtful. Thank you, Mrs. Devon. I hope it is not an imposition—"

"Not at all." The married woman beamed at them both, so Robert returned her smile, though it faltered when he caught his employer's somewhat intense stare. Had Devon seen him holding Miss Clark's wrist? Had he appeared threatening or merely overly familiar? Whatever the case, Robert had no intention of giving any reason for Devon to question him on it.

Devon's suspicious stare turned somewhat sly. "You will have to stay as well, Ellsworth."

Robert's response sounded strained even to his own ears. "That is not necessary, Mr. Devon. My house is nearly upon your own property. I could make it there in a blizzard and remain safe enough."

Mrs. Devon looked between Robert and her husband, then at Penny. "It only makes sense, Mr. Ellsworth. If we keep one of our dinner guests, we ought to keep the other."

Despite his protests, the couple insisted—Devon with an expression that said he guessed entirely too well about Robert's thoughts on the lovely Miss Clark. When dinner was announced, Robert took Mrs. Devon into the table while Penny was escorted by Mr. Devon. After all were seated and made the appropriate comments regarding the loveliness of the table, Devon brought the conversation around to a subject no one seemed capable of avoiding: the weather.

"Ellsworth and I have ridden out to the eastern meadows twice this week, to check the pond and the stream it feeds between our property and the Gilbert estate. The water is far past its usual boarders. I fear, before long, we may have a great deal of trouble in the village."

The lady of the house examined her husband carefully, as though attempting to determine his level of concern before deciding on her own. "It was all anyone talked about yesterday, when we delivered the baskets and good tidings. I rode with Father, Miss Clark with the curate, but we all had similar conversations."

Whoever made the assignments for delivery partners had obviously been making an attempt at matchmaking. The curate had courted Mrs. Devon, or Miss Ames two years ago, and been rejected in favor of Harry Devon. Everyone knew the story. Yet the curate had proven a man not prone to hold a grudge and carried on quite amicably in the community, despite his romantic disappointment.

Though he hated to admit it to himself, or out loud, Robert had to make some comment on the matter. What had Penny thought of the curate? "Mr. Haskett escorted you, Miss Clark?"

Penny looked across the small table at him, the usual brightness in her features dimmed. "Yes, he did. He is a very fine gentleman, courteous and kind. He obviously cares a great deal for everyone in the community. He soothed as many fears as he could, but many families are expecting hardship to result from all this rain. Several are already blaming illnesses upon the weather, and nearly everyone beseeched Mr. Haskett to keep praying for an end to it."

Guilt at his own selfish reason for the line of conversation momentarily stinged Robert's heart. He silently begged forgiveness for allowing jealousy to creep in, turning his attention to his plate rather than to Penny. "As we all should pray for an end to this weather, before more serious harm comes from it."

"The London papers all tell of flooding. Dams breaking." Mrs. Devon touched a hand to her forehead. "I wish there were a way to help. I cannot remember the weather ever being this terrible. I worry for the children especially. They grow ill, and they suffer—whether they are the children of London's streets or the little ones in our village trapped in drafty houses."

For a time after Mrs. Devon spoke, the only sound any of them heard was that of rain upon the windows.

"I am grateful you allowed me to stay this evening," Penny said, her voice breaking the silence in her humble thanks. "I do not enjoy traveling in such a downpour as this. I am afraid rain makes me rather nervous."

"Then this must be a trying time for you," Mrs. Devon said sympathetically. "I am pleased you agreed to stay. We will enjoy our meal together and retire to the parlor. Truly, it will be a great treat to have you. Poor Harry has had to content himself with only me for conversation and entertainment for such a long time." Her eyes sparkled as she looked at her husband, sharing a smile with him that held more meaning than Robert could understand.

His gaze moved to Penny to see if she had noted the couple's warm exchange, only to find her already watching him. One corner of her mouth tipped upward as though to say, *I do not think they mind each other's company in the least.*

Robert chuckled and hid the sound by clearing his throat.

Casting a frown at him, Devon leaned over the table. "Are you all right, Ellsworth?"

With a hasty nod, Robert took up his cup and swallowed, pretending to have experienced a food difficulty.

Penny lowered her eyes and raised a linen square to cover her mouth, her shoulders shaking enough for him to know she struggled to stifle her own laughter, likely at Robert's expense.

When the conversation safely turned to another topic, he found himself wishing for Penny's eyes to return to him once more. When they finally did, there was a somewhat playful apology within them for the ruckus she had caused. They had almost always known what the other was thinking in childhood. Knowing that they still had that much of a connection, even if it had resurfaced at an odd moment, wrapped Robert's heart in warm contentment. No matter how they had grown, no matter their current circumstances, they were yet the closest of friends.

CHAPTER 10

After dinner, everyone adjourned to the parlor. The gentlemen had already spent the entire day working together, it seemed, and thus had no reason to remain behind for the purpose of business. Penny would have been disappointed if this were the case. Every additional moment in Robert's company was another thing to be grateful for, especially knowing she would leave him behind again soon enough.

The group settled into the same comfortable parlor where Mrs. Devon and Penny had chatted away the afternoon, reliving their shared childhood with fondness. The women had delighted in exchanging those memories for nearly an hour. The only ones left unspoken were the ones of the boy Robert, the ones that had involuntarily flooded into Penny's mind. He had always been there.

A part of Penny had hoped—had held onto the girl-hood dream—of becoming more than a friend to him. But it was not to be. Not if he had his eyes and heart set upon another. What was she to do? With her brothers leaving to make their way in the world, and her aunt and uncle's own children grown and doing the same, Penny could not allow herself to depend upon their kindness for much longer.

"How is it," Mr. Devon asked politely, "that the three of you knew each other so well, yet I never came to know any of you better than a nodding acquaintance?"

Daisy Devon positioned herself on the couch next to her husband, giving his arm a conciliatory pat. "Your father had no wish for you to mix with the locals, darling. We could not possibly aid you in attaining the greatness he hoped for you."

"True enough," Robert agreed with a crooked smirk. "You also attended the wrong school, you know."

"One would say *you* attended the wrong school," Harry said with a similar smug grin. Obviously, the gentlemen had made a habit of jesting with each other on whose educational institution was the better of the two— Harrow or Eton.

"You men and your schools. You do not hear Miss Clark and I arguing over which of us is the better scholar or seamstress." Daisy nudged her husband in the shoulder, fondly rebuking him.

The window behind her told of the rain still pattering at a quick pace, and storms often left her distracted; but from her place in a chair near the fire, Penny observed the married couple with greater interest. Everything about Daisy, the way she turned toward her husband, her hand remaining upon his arm, and the fondness in her gaze, spoke of contentment and comfort. Penny had once hoped to obtain something like that for herself.

"You ladies are certainly above such behavior. We are

not at all worthy of your company," Mr. Devon said, looking with equal tenderness upon his wife.

From the corner of her eye, Penny watched Robert as he sat in the chair nearest her own. Only a small, circular table separated them. She had much preferred when nothing had stood between them, as when they had shared the larger piece of furniture on the other side of the Persian rug. But such closeness would never do. Hoping he might take up her hand, as he had momentarily held her wrist in his gentle grasp, was foolish.

"I would not go so far as that," Daisy said, looking rather as though she wished to tuck herself closer to her husband and forget they had guests. Instead, she abruptly addressed Penny. "Miss Clark, do tell my husband what you think of my idea to start a school for girls. You are uniquely situated to explain to him how it would be of benefit to more than just the children."

"A school for girls?" Robert leaned back in his chair, crossing his legs before him in a somewhat casual manner. "You mean the school where you currently teach, in the village?"

Daisy had told Penny all about her efforts to educate the daughters of the local tradesmen and farmers. Several days a week, the morning school would meet within the village itself. Although the school would not start again until after Epiphany, Daisy adored her scholars and already planned upon taking on more.

"Something like that," Daisy answered. "Only larger, allowing for more students and less of the work laid upon my own shoulders. There is a vast deal to do, and I cannot accomplish it all alone. Especially with the household to run, and our expectation for a child of our own in the spring."

Most would not discuss such a blessed event before company, but it only made sense that Robert would be aware of the increase of his employer's household, and Penny had been told only a few hours previous that Daisy expected her first child in March. Perhaps that explained a great deal of the warm glow in Daisy's eyes. One often heard that women in the family way tended to have an extra touch of gentleness about them, something magic and secretive.

Robert took her from her suppositions when he turned to face her from his chair, leaning slightly in her direction. "And why are you uniquely situated for this conversation, Miss Clark?" He gave her a teasing smile, though she detected the barest hint of curiosity in his dark eyes.

Oh. She had not intended to tell Robert directly of her future plans. And especially not like this. "I suppose because I intend to try my luck at obtaining a position at a girls' school." She offered him a tight smile, the sort that begged him not to ask too many questions here. Though she had already explained the situation to Daisy, she would rather speak to Robert in private of her decision to work.

The way his smile faltered, his brows drawing together, immediately caused her shoulders to stiffen. What would he think of her, turning to employment? Nothing too terrible, she hoped, given that he had also entered into a world wherein he depended upon work for his income.

Neither of them had been raised to seek out such positions, but plans had a way of changing at times. She couldn't decipher the look on Robert's face.

"That would give you a unique perspective," Mr. Devon said, and when she turned her attention to him, she noted with curiosity that he looked to Robert, not to her.

"Yes. I have a great many hopes, of course, for the sort of position I wish to obtain. I am fortunate that I have time to consider my opportunities, too. I need not take the first position offered or the first school I apply to if it does not suit me. Yet I am determined to find a place before summer. My aunt and uncle have supported me since my parents' death, but I cannot rely upon them forever."

At last Mr. Devon took his gaze away from his employee in order to settle a kind smile upon her. "I greatly respect your desire to make your way in the world. You have obviously discussed the matter with my wife, but what can you tell me about your opinion of a school for the middle and working classes? Daisy is adamant that a larger school for such young ladies would be a success."

"It would be more modest than what is offered for the daughters of gentlemen and nobility," Daisy quickly added.

Penny had given the matter some thought. "I do believe many parents would sacrifice for their girls, if they could. Sons can be apprenticed, or go to local schools run by the church, but daughters of that particular background have more limited options. They are expected to do all their helping and learning at home. I know there are other schools such as what you are suggesting, Mrs.

Devon. I have seen many advertisements for them in my search for a position."

Robert made a noise, a sort of surprised mumble, but when he did not attempt to actually speak, Penny continued. "If I could obtain a position at such a school, knowing I was to help teach girls with less privileged backgrounds and upbringing than myself, I should like it. I do not require much in terms of salary, thanks to the small inheritance left to me, but others might not be willing to teach if they are not compensated as well as they would be at a larger school. You would still wish for accomplished teachers, after all, and not only those who were unable to take up a place at a more demanding and prestigious institution."

"Well said." Mr. Devon regarded her frankly, studying her without a smile or amusement. "This is precisely what my concern is. Though I care for all my wife's endeavors, we ourselves cannot fund every school she wishes to begin. We are already in support of two institutions in London—"

"Ragged schools," Daisy added helpfully.

"—and the school Daisy runs here, as well as several scholarships for the children of Annesbury who wish to go on to more formal universities."

"There are two young men training to become doctors in Edinburgh," Robert said, joining the conversation for the first time since Penny's answer seemed to have thrown him. "One of them has agreed to come back to Annesbury after he completes his training, the other intends to apprentice himself to Mr. Devon's brother-in-law, in Bath. They are doing quite well."

Daisy took her husband's hand and turned to look into

his eyes, her own expression fervent. "And still, I wish I could do more."

To Penny's surprise, Mr. Devon lifted his wife's hand to his lips and placed a kiss upon her knuckles. Such an affectionate display was not something she had commonly seen in married couples of her acquaintance.

"One of the many things I love about you is your desire to bring education to everyone who wishes for it," Mr. Devon said, smiling as his wife's cheeks pinkened. "We will keep working, my dear, to do all we can."

The conversation drifted away to other topics, but Penny found it more difficult to contribute than before. The warmth between the married couple, the obvious regard they held for each other, had put her into a thoughtful frame of mind difficult to escape. What would it be like to be doted upon in such a way? To be loved and supported so wholly, just for being one's self? She continued to wander down that path, her attention only occasionally catching hold of the conversation at hand.

"Mrs. Devon, are you certain we cannot persuade you to reveal the characters you will have at your masque?" Robert asked at one point in the evening. "How is one to plan a costume without sufficient notice?"

The woman raised one eyebrow most imperiously. "I have no intention of telling anyone, not even you, Mr. Ellsworth, of what I plan. You will receive your assignment two days prior and not a moment before. That ought to keep everyone's identity a mystery."

"We know you will only appeal to your housekeeper for help with your costume," Mr. Devon said, a smug tilt to his chin. "But I have seen my wife's list, and even made a few suggestions. I think you will be satisfied."

"It sounds as though you have reason to fear, Robert." Penny could not resist joining the teasing, forgetting herself a moment and using his Christian name as though they were not in company. "When your employer and his wife conspire against you for your role at a masque."

At that, Mr. Devon put on the most alarming grin. "Oh, we have your costume decided upon as well, Miss Clark."

Daisy settled in more, snuggling against her husband. "Decided only this evening, in fact."

"That is hardly comforting." Penny laughed around the words. "And I cannot prevail upon you for even a hint?"

Robert tapped the arm of his chair. "Here now, if I am to be kept ignorant, so too should you. We will have to trust that Mrs. Devon is a kind soul who will not humiliate us at her party." He put on an expression of pleading, his eyes wide and his smile playfully pained.

Daisy laughed. "I promise nothing, except that I will do my best to avoid any embarrassment for either of you." She brushed aside the topic and asked, "How are your brothers doing at present, Mr. Ellsworth? Especially Peter with his studies."

Penny stole a glance at Robert, while he spoke with some animation about his younger brother's schooling. She longed to know which woman had captured his romantic attention, for she would happily berate the lady for not understanding what a treasure she had in Robert Ellsworth. Whoever that woman was, did she not know how Robert would adore her? Would make her laugh and smile, would speak to her as an equal?

If Penny could not have her heart's desire, Robert ought to have his. Perhaps, if she could discover the mystery woman's identity, Penny could help Robert's cause.

Her heart ached at it, but her mind latched onto that plan. Long after everyone bid each other goodnight, and she retired to her guest room, she remained awake, wondering how she might help her dearest friend.

CHAPTER 11

After a quiet breakfast, Robert made his petition for the honor of escorting Penny and her maid back to the Brody home. "The Brodys reside on the other side of Annesbury, and I have business matters in town. I can see Miss Clark safely there and handle the estate affairs on my return." He sat across the table from Penny, with Devon at the head. Mrs. Devon had sent word that she did not feel well and would take her breakfast in her room.

Devon agreed without hesitation. "I would appreciate that kindness, if you do not mind, Miss Clark?"

"Of course not." Penny lowered her fork, a sparkle appearing in her eye. "Mr. Ellsworth will be an excellent escort. If you both will excuse me, I will make certain I am ready to depart."

Robert watched her leave, and his chest grew tighter when she turned to smile over her shoulder just before closing the door. Every moment spent in her company made his heart and soul ache. Why he kept seeking out that sort of pain was a mystery to him. He brought his attention back to his coffee. As he sipped from his cup, however, he spotted Devon grinning at him over the rim.

"You, dear fellow, need to tell that woman how you feel about her."

Whether he gasped or choked, Robert was not sure, but the result was the same. Hot coffee went through his throat in the wrong direction and for an agonizing moment he could not breathe. He covered his mouth with a handkerchief and coughed, his eyes watering. Only this time it was not pretend.

Devon only crossed his arms over his chest, appearing completely unconcerned that Robert had nearly expired at the breakfast table. "You are not fooling anyone. Daisy and I are in agreement, based upon our observations yesterday, that you are in love with Miss Clark."

Robert shook his head, overcoming the coughing fit at last. "You are mistaken. Miss Clark, she is not— I could not have such feelings for her."

"As a man who nearly lost his opportunity with the love of his life, I call your bluff, sir, and insist that you do something about your affections before Miss Clark leaves you behind to go teach at a girls' school." Devon tossed his own linen to the table as he stood. "If you will excuse me, I wish to see to my wife." He gave Robert a firm pat on the shoulder as he walked by. "Good luck, Ellsworth."

He folded his arms and dropped his face into them, though he kept in the groan that, if emitted, would have summed up his feelings on the matter. What had Devon seen? As long as Penny had not glimpsed his thoughts, had no guess at his feelings, they might still be friends.

He rose from his place at the table and went to gather his coat, hat, and gloves. Awaiting Penny in the entryway would be the best way for him to spend his time. He could worry over whether or not she had caught him out later.

Penny did not keep him waiting long. The maid who had accompanied her on her visit followed behind, expression pleasant but noninvasive.

"This is Anna, a maid from the Brody household who received far more trouble than she bargained for when she set out with me yesterday."

"Weren't any trouble, miss," the smiling Anna said with a lilt in her voice. "M'sister is a kitchen maid here, and we had a good enough time tradin' news." The young woman appeared rather as though she had enjoyed a holiday rather than a night of uncertainty.

Penny adjusted the scarf around her neck, the bold red of the fabric complimenting the pink in her cheeks. "Are you ready to leave, Robert?"

"I am. The coach is waiting for us, too."

Mr. Devon's voice called to them from the top of the stairs. They turned to see him coming down at a quick pace, but countenance he wore reassured Robert nothing was amiss. "I am come with my wife's regrets that she cannot bid you farewell this morning. We enjoyed your company, Miss Clark. And Robert, you need not hurry back to your duties. I am certain there are things you should see to at your own home. Please, take your time."

At that, Robert and Penny bid him farewell, and Robert led the way outside to the carriage. The gravel drive of the Devon home had not been overcome with water or mud, but there was a fair chance the rest of the roads did not weather the storms as easily.

After he handed Penny and the maid into the back of the coach, Robert took the seat with his back to the driver and swung the door shut. The cold had returned, making the warm bricks beneath their feet an added blessing. The women had pulled a thick blanket over their laps, too.

They had barely started on their way when Penny started to speak, almost in a rush, as though trying to cover the silence with words. "Daisy is every bit as kind and personable as ever, I am pleased to say. I always thought her kind when we played together, though it did not happen nearly so often as you keeping me company. Strange, is it not, that I would spend more time with a boy of my age than a girl? She did always live on the other side of the village, though, so that does explain some of the lack."

Robert tilted his hat back a touch, allowing him a better view of her. Penny sat with her hands in her lap, resting upon the blanket, her fingers twisting about each other. Was she nervous about something?

"I always liked her, too. Devon married well. They are a match for one another, both kind and generous souls." He studied his friend closely, watching the way her eyes darted from the floor of the carriage to the glass windows, never settling long anywhere.

She bit her bottom lip, then eyed the silent maid who stared out her own window in polite boredom. Finally, she met Robert's stare directly. "It is good they have found one another. Not everyone is so blessed to meet their match, and in such circumstances where they might have time to know for a certainty that they belong together. I know I have not done so, though I did try at one time."

"I admit, I found it surprising that you had not yet wed." Though it might not be the sort of conversation most gentlemen would have with a female acquaintance,

Robert knew Penny well enough that he knew she would not think he slighted her. "I always thought, once you had your come out, that you would be a success in that arena."

Her light laugh, the way her eyes crinkled at the corners, told him he had not erred in guessing her ease with the subject. "I appreciate the compliment, Robert. Though you and I both know that it is more than a pretty face most gentleman look for. I have no title, no connections of value, and a very small dowry. Unless a gentleman nurtured a strong affection for me, I have no hope of securing a husband."

There was no bitterness in her tone, not sharpness in her words. She did not even appear the least sorry for her situation. She had come to peace with the idea of remaining unmarried, most obviously.

"That is why you look for a position as a teacher?" he asked, trying to picture her in a role he had always thought for much older and less pleasant women. The carriage rumbled along at a slow, steady pace. In the distance, he heard thunder. The thought of still more rain nearly made him cross.

Penny's eyes went to the window again, and he thought he caught her tense up. "The idea of teaching is more appealing than living upon the kindness of my relatives, as I have done since my parents' death."

"Has it been difficult, to live with the Marhams?" Something of his surprise must have leaked into his tone, for she immediately returned her gaze to him.

"Not at all. Aunt Elizabeth and Uncle Matthew are kind, and most generous with all their time and attention. But my brothers have left to seek their living, and I wish to do the same. Though I would be employed as a teacher, there would be a measure of independence I have yet to enjoy."

"Ah, I see." Perhaps his unique situation lent him a better insight into her decision than most. His father's prolonged illness, as well as poor investment and management decisions before Samuel had realized the seriousness of their father's condition, had left their family in difficult financial straits. His position with the Devons had helped more than anyone knew. "I hope you find a position that is all you desire." Would being the wife of a steward be less worthy of her than a teaching position? It might not afford the same level of independence she wished.

She gave him a more tentative smile than usual. "Thank you, Robert." Then her hands went back to twisting about each other. "I am hopeful that you have found joy in your position, too. A steward carries a great deal of responsibility. Hearing what little I did of your discussion with Mr. Devon proves what I suspected when I learned of your work. Your organized and practical mind is perfectly suited for all you must do in the course of your employment."

Though the compliment felt sincere, Robert shrugged it away. "I find a certain satisfaction in what I do." She must not see that his employment was beneath him and her both. He tried not to sigh, instead adjusting his hat back to where it had been before, lower upon his brow. "What are your plans for the New Year? Have the Brodys' special entertainment planned for your visit?"

With that the subject was changed, and Robert did not allow the conversation to stray to the matter of employment again.

CHAPTER 12

The ladies of the Gilbert family met every fortnight, and as Mrs. Brody had once been Miss Martha Gilbert, she invited her guests to join her for the traditional visit to her family's home. The matriarch of the family everyone called Mrs. Gilbert, her daughter-in-law became Christine, and Martha dropped her husband's surname as well.

After the introductions were made, the ladies settled in a parlor with a large window overlooking the gardens and the roof of the stables in the distance.

"I do hope we are not intruding," Aunt Elizabeth said, taking up her sewing. "It is most kind of you to allow us to be part of your family gathering for the day."

Christine poured tea near the window and answered for her family. "It is always a pleasure to host friends, and Martha has told us so much about you, Mrs. Marham."

"Do please call me Elizabeth," she said brightly. It was quickly agreed upon that the women would know each other by their Christian names, at least for the course of the sewing gathering.

While it certainly pleased Penny to be included, she had her own plans. Yet, she attended to the surrounding conversation, listening to Aunt Elizabeth, Martha Brody, and Christine Gilbert discuss the merits of certain needles, their current sewing projects, and the possibility of piecing together a new quilt. Finally, Mrs. Christine Gilbert spoke on a subject that would do for Penny to enact her plan.

"What did you ladies think of the kissing balls at the earl's Christmas Ball? I confess, I was surprised by the sheer number of them. There must have been a dozen, each with a dozen silver berries." Her smile turned somewhat mischievously. "My husband claimed one fairly early in the evening."

Mrs. Brody adjusted the spectacles on her nose she had taken from her sewing basket. She peered over the wire frame. "I saw a great many matrons turning their noses up, while at the same time herding their daughters beneath the mistletoe. I have never been so entertained."

Though it was not precisely the way Penny wished to begin, she seized the opportunity. Keeping her fingers busy with her embroidery, head down, she said, "I was the recipient of a mistletoe kiss."

The other ladies shifted, and Aunt Elizabeth dropped her sewing into her lap. "Penelope, you did not say a word to me about it. Dear me. Whoever was bold enough to take a kiss from a young woman so newly returned to the neighborhood?"

"I am certain I could guess," Mrs. Brody said, one corner of her mouth going upward.

"Oh, it was only Robert Ellsworth." Penny lifted one shoulder in a shrug, not even smiling over the memory. She did not wish to be the subject of the teasing, but to discuss Robert. "We are very good friends, and always have been. His elder brother goaded him into it." She doubted he had even bothered to take a berry, the traditional trophy of a young man who had won a Christmas kiss.

Christine Gilbert scoffed, tossing her head in a way that made her brown curls dance beneath her white cap. "No man can be forced into kissing a woman he does not already wish to kiss. I am certain your Mr. Ellsworth enjoyed the moment."

Although heat burned at the top of her cheeks, Penny ignored the sensation. "Oh, perhaps, but I know that he has his eye on another young lady. I think he might have given his kiss with greater enthusiasm had I been that particular person."

Mrs. Brody and her sister-in-law exchanged wide-eyed glances. "Truly?" Mrs. Brody asked. "I had not heard of him forming any sort of attachment."

"Nor have I. Though it is not necessarily my business to know of such things," Christine Gilbert said, "I am certain my brother would have mentioned it. Mr. Robert Ellsworth is my brother's steward," she explained when Aunt Elizabeth's brow furrowed.

"Dear me. I was not aware of that connection." Aunt Elizabeth tipped her head to one side, eyeing Penny with a slight frown. Oh dear. Aunt Elizabeth appeared most suspicious.

Penny hurried to move the conversation along. "I am under the impression that Robert has not yet secured the young lady's good opinion, though he must be hopeful of doing so. We only spoke on the subject briefly. I have been away from the neighborhood so long, though, that I am not much help to him. I cannot even be sure which miss he has his eye upon."

"If I think on it, I might determine whom it might be." Christine pursed her lips. She was an elegant woman in appearance, though Penny had always been rather intimidated by her. The woman had a fierce sort of boldness that she never feared to display. Penny had been younger than all three Devon sisters, so she had always been a bit in awe of them.

After another moment of silence, Aunt Elizabeth spoke again. "I have heard a great deal about Mr. Ellsworth, before we even came to visit. He and Penny were apparently thick as thieves before she and her brothers came to live with us. I do not think I have heard a single childhood memory mentioned by Penny without a mention of 'Robert did this,' or 'Robert said that.'"

Penny accidentally stabbed her thumb with her needle and yelped, putting the injured finger to her lips. She blinked rapidly, staring up at her aunt.

"Oh, you poor dear," the elder Mrs. Gilbert said sympathetically. "Here. Let me have your handkerchief. I will wet it for you and you may wrap your thumb in it." She came and retrieved Penny's handkerchief and went to the tea things.

"Are you all right?" Aunt Elizabeth asked, real surprise upon her face. "I cannot remember the last time you hurt yourself with a needle. You are usually so deft at your sewing."

Loathe to confirm whatever suspicions her aunt had

begun to form, Penny cast about for an excuse and found one out the window. "It is the weather, I am afraid. It has me all out of sorts."

Aunt Elizabeth's features softened, her eyes filling with sympathy. "My poor dear. Yes, I imagine all the rain and thunder would strain your nerves. I know all the gray clouds and damp have brought my spirits low a time or two."

The other women in the room murmured their agreement, and wishes for sunshine or even snow, anything to end the monotony of rainfall. But Aunt Elizabeth reached out and gave Penny's uninjured hand a gentle squeeze, which made Penny duck her head in guilt.

Aunt Elizabeth assumed the weather had caused Penny to dwell on the night she lost her parents to a rainstorm and poorly maintained bridge, which would of course prove distressing. In truth, Penny's thoughts and heart had been turned too often in Robert's direction to give her time to think on what she had lost years before. Yes, the pain of her parents' deaths would always be with her, but the old ache had lessened somewhat since the moment she laid eyes upon Robert beneath his umbrella.

Unfortunately, the conversation turned to other topics, such as the coming New Year's Eve festivities, the masque ball, and Epiphany itself. Nothing else was said about Robert, and Mrs. Christine Gilbert never brought up whether she had thought of a likely candidate for his affection.

R obert arrived late to the New Year's Eve party at the Brody home. Frankly, when he received an invitation he had been surprised. He did not know the Brody family particularly well, but if they wished to invite people to make Penny comfortable, he supposed the invitation made sense. When he entered the house, which was nearly as fine as the Devon estate, he shook droplets of water from his hat before handing it to the butler.

Once Robert's overcoat had been taken, the butler handed everything off to a footman. "This way, Mr. Ellsworth. The guests are in the drawing room." The butler led the way up the wide steps and through a corridor until they arrived at a pair of doors. From behind the doors, Robert heard laughter, and someone playing the pianoforte.

He drew in a breath, settling his nerves, preparing to lay eyes upon Penny for the first time since he took her home. The butler opened the doors and announced Robert's arrival.

Mr. George Brody appeared immediately at Robert's side, bowing. "Mr. Robert Ellsworth, so good of you to come. Your brothers are already here." He gestured to a corner of the room where a large pianoforte stood, Samuel and Peter standing on either side of its player. Of course, the one playing was none other than Penny.

"I am grateful for the invitation, Mr. Brody. Thank you for including me in your celebration of the New Year."

"Not at all, sir." Brody grinned broadly at Robert. "We will play games soon, and of course have a round of snapdragon and cake. We mean to go down to the entry to let the New Year in, too. All the best traditions and none of the dull nonsense." Brody gestured to the room again. "Please, make yourself comfortable and enjoy the evening."

With his brothers flanking Penny at the instrument, Robert knew exactly where he wished to begin his evening. He made his way to the corner of the room, stopping on occasion to trade nods with other guests. His focus remained entirely on Penny, though she had not yet noticed his entrance. She had her hair up upon her head like a crown, woven through with white ribbons, and pearls at her throat. She wore an ivory dress, capturing the look of a perfect angel.

Her eyes rose from her music and met his when he was only a few steps away, and the notes of the song faltered. Had he startled her? But then, her smile, the one she seemed to save just for him, turned the corners of her mouth upward and made her eyes twinkle. As he took in this brief loveliness, he couldn't help but remember the special look Mrs. Devon had for her husband. Strange that it almost felt comparable.

"Here is Robert, come to answer all of our questions about him." A hint of teasing in her tone was all the warning he had before Samuel turned a somewhat conniving grin in his direction.

"Ah, the middle brother. We have had the most entertaining conversation about you."

Peter appeared almost delighted by Robert's arrival, though he made a valiant effort to temper his grin. "I'm not certain Robert will be as amused as we are by our speculations."

Penny winced, her expression one of chagrin. "I am afraid I am to blame for this, Robert. I thought I asked a perfectly innocent question, but now your brothers are rather like hounds on the scent of a fox."

"Whatever do you mean?" Robert asked, noting Samuel's unchanged grin from the corner of his eye.

After one last flourish of notes, Penny removed her hands from the instrument keys and placed them in her lap. She narrowed her eyes at Samuel. "Do stop that, Samuel. You look like you are contemplating something wicked."

"Oh, I think he is," Peter said, rocking forward on his heels and back again. "And I would rather not be present for it." He bowed, somewhat sharply, then walked away. "Good luck, Rob," he tossed over his shoulder.

Robert needed to face the issue head on and get to the bottom of it. Though Penny appeared somewhat anxious, Samuel's obvious satisfaction needed addressing. "Out with it, Sam. I have the feeling we cannot enjoy our evening until you have your fun."

Samuel cut a glance at Penny before tucking his hands behind his back and lifting his eyebrows superciliously.

"Our charming friend, Miss Clark, has asked me if I thought you might have a mind to court a certain young woman."

Warmth suffused him, creeping up his neck and into his ears. Nothing had prepared Robert for that. Indeed, his heart skipped about like a startled deer before Samuel had even finished speaking. Robert swallowed, though the action did nothing to subdue the excitement in that moment.

Had Penny noticed—did she suspect—that Robert nurtured feelings for her? Is that why she asked Samuel such a bold question? Perhaps she had hoped for a hint—

The woman he loved spoke rapidly, her words almost defensive. "I had no idea that Samuel would treat the question as a subject for jest and wild speculation. I merely wondered if you had your eye on any young lady so that I might be certain I approved. You know I could not countenance you wedding someone I could not enjoy visiting." She tipped her chin up and narrowed her coppery eyes first at Samuel, then at Robert. "I apologize that my curiosity has set your brother on this fox chase."

Her words doused his hope as easily as a pail of water would douse a candle. Then she had not hoped to hear, had not even thought it possible, that it was she whom he wished to pay court.

"A fox chase?" Samuel asked, obviously unaware of the turn in Robert's mood. The eldest Ellsworth sounded as merry as ever. "I do not think I should have to run far to find a young lady that would make my brother a happy partner, and likely fulfill whatever standard you wish of her, Miss Clark." He put a hand on Robert's shoulder and tried to share his good humor, too. "What say you,

Robert? Will this be the last year you spend as a bachelor?"

Though he wished to pull away, to bow coldly and leave without another word, Robert could not do that to Penny. She did not understand her innocent desire had wounded him. But Samuel ought to have known better than to mock the situation, considering that he suspected Robert's heart already had a favorite in Penny Clark.

Forcing a grin, Robert shrugged just enough to remove Samuel's hand. "I have no intention of finding a wife, Sam, as you well know. My hours are too devoted to my duties to consider courtship. Though I thank you both for your concern."

With a snort, Samuel started to argue. "But Rob—"

"I think," Penny said, cutting him off as she stood from the pianoforte, "that I should like some punch." She came to stand between the brothers and looked from one to the other. "Who will attend me to the refreshment table in the other room?"

Samuel, who had frozen the moment she stood, closed his mouth with a click. He quickly bowed. "As I have already had the pleasure of your company for the last quarter hour, I will allow my brother that honor."

Of course he would. Traitor. Doing everything he could to humiliate Robert for the feelings he held for Penny. Robert glared at Samuel over her head and spoke through gritted teeth. "It would be my pleasure, Penny."

She took his arm and tugged until he fell in step beside her, making for the door. Across the room a door connected to another room where more guests milled near a large table well-laden with platters, bowls, and cups of every sort of refreshment one could wish for a celebration. They walked in that direction, Robert's heart contracting painfully when he saw the concern in Penny's eyes.

"I had not meant to cause you distress, Robert," she whispered to him as they moved through the guests. "When you admitted there was someone, I let my curiosity overcome my good sense. But I only wished to help, truly."

Robert shook his head, allowing his shoulders to fall as he let out a breathy laugh. "Help? How could your curiosity help me, Penny?"

A flash of hurt appeared, or so he thought, before she lowered her eyes to the floor. They had crossed the threshold into the next room when she answered. "I thought, if I knew whom you admired, I might better encourage you, or even speak to the lady of all your wonderful traits. I had no well-thought-out plan. But I desire your happiness."

As he desired hers.

"Your motivation was kind," he acknowledged. "Please, Penny. Do not trouble yourself on my account. I am a man grown, or had you not noticed?" He attempted a smile, but his lips fell flat almost immediately. "I am a steward. Not a fine catch."

"That is preposterous. I wish you could see that." Penny released his arm to take up a cup of punch. She handed the first to him, then took another for herself to sip. She turned away, allowing him an unimpeded view of her lovely profile. After she lowered her cup, she released a breath full of displeasure. "Robert, you are a wonderful man. Any woman would be well-pleased to have your attention."

"Even you?" was what he wanted to ask. Rather than risk his mouth releasing the question, he gulped down his punch in one long swig. When he finished, he put the cup down on a tray for a servant to remove to the kitchens.

Penny regarded him with a puzzled expression, and her lips parted as though to ask a question, but Mr. Brody called the room to order. His two-dozen guests turned their attention to their host, including Penny. Robert allowed his eyes to linger on her another moment, wondering what she would have said, watching her lips press together again and trying not to remember the mistletoe kiss. Or the fact that the silver berry he had claimed still rested in his waistcoat pocket. He'd taken to carrying it about with him, as though it were a talisman or charm against ill luck.

He called himself a fool and yielded his attention to Mr. Brody's announcement.

"We are to play snapdragon! Make certain to remove your gloves and only play if you believe yourself to have nimble fingers." He gestured for the servants to bring a table forward, then two footmen brought out a large copper platter. Maids poured pitchers of brandy into the shallow basin, and then raisins were sprinkled inside by Mrs. Brody.

Penny bobbed up and down on her heels, the earlier concern on her face replaced by an expression of childlike glee. "Oh, I do love this game." The lamps lit around the room were dimmed, candles blown out, and then Mr. Brody lit the brandy.

Blue and purple flames sprung up in the bowl, dancing eerily in the darkness.

"Who will claim the most raisins, I wonder?" Mrs.

Brody asked the room, the challenge and laughter both in her voice.

Penny had already stripped the glove from her right hand and moved forward eagerly, and Robert came behind her. Several guests stayed back, in the shadowed edges of the room, speaking quietly and laughing as others tried their luck. Peter had three raisins out and popped in his mouth before he yelped and backed away. A young lady managed two. Samuel took only one before shaking his hand out and standing aside to allow two other guests to take his place.

Then Penny and Robert both stood at the table, and Robert belatedly remembered to remove his glove.

"Shall we go at the same time?" Penny asked, and he saw the blue flames reflected in her eyes. Had there ever been a woman as lovely as she? Surely, never.

"Yes. We'll go at the same time and then again. First to falter owes the other a forfeit," he said, the silver berry in his pocket seeming to press against him.

Mrs. Brody heard the remark and called it out to others in the room. "We have a contest between Mr. Robert Ellsworth and Miss Clark. Let us see who loses their nerve first." Others in the room clapped, a few calling out their encouragement.

"You can best him, Miss Clark," shouted Samuel from somewhere behind them.

Penny's hand went forward and Robert hurried to match her, snatching a raisin from the burning pan at the same moment she did. The flames licked at his wrist but did not burn. Then they reached in again and each pulled out a second raisin. Then a third. Penny moved with a quickness he could not hope to match for long. Fourth raisins were freed from fire and eaten, warm and beginning to plump with brandy.

A glance at Penny from the corner of his eye revealed her tongue darting out to lick a drop of brandy from her lips, and Robert faltered. Her hand was already in the bowl when he finally moved to catch up, barely popping the fruit into his mouth before reaching for another—

They both reached for the same raisin, their fingers tangling a moment, hands colliding, and the brief hesitation it caused in both their movements sent the blue flames flickering over their hands, turning orange. Penny yipped in pain, snatching her hand back to cradle it against her chest. Robert had the raisin but closed his fist around it and shook out his hand, trying to alleviate the burning sensation.

"Oh dear," Mrs. Brody rushed forward, putting her hand on Penny's shoulder. "Are you injured?"

"No. Not terribly." Penny laughed and nodded to Robert. "But my pride is stung. Did you win the sixth raisin, Mr. Ellsworth?"

He opened his hand to show her in the dim light. "I did."

"We have our winner," Mr. Brody announced, and the room erupted in good-natured laughter and applause.

"Here. Allow me to help you, my dear," Mrs. Brody said quietly, taking Penny aside.

Robert hurried around the table to them. "Allow me, Mrs. Brody. I am afraid I sustained a small burn, too. I can assist Miss Clark and see to my injury at the same time."

"I am certain I will be fine," Penny insisted.

There was more cheering as Peter and another boy near his age began nipping raisins from the fire-lit bowl.

Robert took advantage of the moment, his hand on Penny's arm, and guided her out of the room into the hall where wall sconces remained lit. Robert drew Penny to the nearest lamp and held her hand up to the light to inspect it.

Her ungloved hand trembled slightly, and he reflexively ran his thumb gently across her palm to soothe her. The first finger on her right hand had a shining red patch near the tip, where she had burned herself. "It likely will blister and be tender for a few days," he murmured softly. His heart pounded within his chest, demanding he pay attention to how close they stood, how the length of her arm pressed against his, and that she smelled of cinnamon and brandy, spicy and sweet all at once.

"What of your burn?" she asked in a whisper. Her hand turned in his, and she stood on her toes to look over his wider palm, her fingers delicately touching his skin. The moment was torturous until she spied the small red spot on his ring finger. "Yours does not look too terrible. Does it hurt?"

Robert swallowed back his emotion, tried to tuck it deep within himself. His beautiful friend, the girl he had once hoped to marry grown into a woman of grace, could not know how much he wished to take her in her arms and kiss her. He would soothe all her pains the rest of her life, if she would only allow it. If it were possible.

"Not terribly," he answered at last, his voice hoarse.

Penny stilled and raised her eyes from studying his hand, meeting his gaze. They stood so close, alone in the hall, no one watching. For a long moment they stared at one another, then she tipped her chin upward and moved a tiny bit closer, her eyes falling half-closed.

"Robert," she said, her voice still whisper-soft.

He bent toward her, heart racing, lips already parting in preparation to take hers up in a kiss.

The door to the drawing room opened, and Robert stepped backward abruptly, while Penny became so rigid as though turned to stone. One of the servants stepped out backward, holding the now-covered snapdragon dish. Another servant followed with a cloth, two more carrying the small table between them. They paid no heed to Robert or Penny who stood there likely appearing somewhat guilty.

Before Robert could turn back to Penny, she walked by him, following the servants to the kitchens. He watched her go, realizing belatedly she must be attending to her burned finger. He took a step back, then another, then turned and went directly down the stairs to the front door. If every time he came near her he made a near fool of himself, almost kissing her, their friendship would not last long.

But—he paused on the steps—Penny had seemed on the verge of kissing him back. He stayed there, between ground and first floor, biting the insides of his cheeks while trying to think through what he ought to do. If he went back, would Samuel continue to torment him with jests? That was nearly reason enough to leave. However, to remain near to Penny gave Robert reason enough to stay.

There were still games to play that might cover the awkward moment between Robert and Penny in the corridor. Charades. Apples in a barrel. The welcoming of the New Year.

Robert turned around, resolved to stay. Whatever the

night brought, being near Penny would finish out the old year happily. He walked up the steps and did not resist the smile that turned his lips upward. Penny had tried to determine which young lady held his favor. That meant, as of yet, she had not realized he spoke of *her* when they had discussed the subject.

Entering the corridor once more, Robert raised his eyebrows when he saw Samuel standing outside the drawing room.

"There you are," Samuel said, a quick grin appearing. "Might I have a word with you, Rob?"

"Of course." Robert mentally fortified himself against the teasing, but when Samuel led the way into another room, dark and without guests, Robert followed curiously. "Sam? Is something wrong?" he asked when Samuel shut the door behind them.

"Yes, something is wrong." Samuel folded his arms, barely visible in the shadows of the room. "Rob, why are you not taking advantage of the hand fate has dealt you? Penelope Clark is right here, now, and unattached."

Robert stepped back against the door, hoping its solid strength would keep him upright for this unnerving conversation. "I am only a steward, Sam. She is the daughter of a gentleman—"

"—and about to become a teacher at a girls' school," Samuel finished impatiently. "A teacher, a governess, is not above your position in any way. Stop acting as though you are an impoverished martyr and do something for your own happiness." Samuel laid a hand on Robert's shoulder, a firm touch that somehow made his words gentler. "You have a stable position. You are an honest man. Court her, wed her, and live happily the rest of your days."

Lungs constricting, Robert shook his head. "I cannot hope—Sam. She may not feel the same. It was so long ago that we dreamed, that we supposed what it would be like…." His voice trailed away, the memory of his last summer with Penny before she went away playing in his mind. Did she remember when they stood next to the pond, skipping stones and speaking of their futures? He had ventured, with what confidence a seventeen-year-old boy could manage, to ask if she might consider courting him when they were old enough. At sixteen, she had enthusiastically said she would.

That was so long ago.

"She would not have asked if you had your eye on a woman if she did not hope to learn you were free of attachment," Samuel said, a stubborn sound to his voice that allowed Robert to easily picture through the dark the glower that must be on his brother's face.

"Do stop," Robert said, then groaned. "I nearly kissed her only a moment ago, in the hall."

"Truly?" Samuel laughed and clapped him on the shoulder harder.

"I see no reason to rejoice over it," Robert muttered, rubbing at the spot his brother had struck with more force than necessary. "Do you not remember what happened when I kissed her at the ball? She ran as though she could not be rid of me fast enough. I have barely restored her trust in me after that incident."

When Samuel spoke again, he sounded chagrinned. "We both know it is my fault she ran. If I had not been present, things may have turned out differently. I am sorry for that, Rob. I promise I will not cause you any more trouble. I will remain firmly out of the way when it comes to Miss Clark."

Samuel could be right. Perhaps Penny had only been uncomfortable due to the public nature of that moment. Robert's own reluctance had been strong, indeed, to act upon Samuel's demands that Penny be kissed. And how incredible it had been, despite everything, to finally have a taste of her lips.

Closing his eyes, tilting his head back to rest against the wall, Robert released a deep-felt, long-suffering sigh. "Let me think on it, Sam."

"Do not think too long. She leaves the day after Epiphany," Samuel reminded him. "You have six days, Robert." Then his brother opened the door, letting enough light into the room that Robert couldn't miss the concern on his elder brother's face. He had such worry in his eyes. "You both deserve happiness, no matter your positions in life." He stepped out, closing the door behind him, leaving Robert alone in the dark with his thoughts.

CHAPTER 14

Penny muttered darkly to herself as she picked her way through the mud, a lamp in one hand and her skirts held above the damp in the other. Although not at all superstitious, when her Aunt Elizabeth reminded her of this particular New Year's tradition, Penny had leaped upon the idea with enthusiasm.

As the last of the guests departed from the Brody house, her aunt had leaned near Penny to whisper, "You ought to go down to the well and get the New Year's cream before someone else thinks to do so."

"Why do men not have traditions this ridiculous?" She grumbled and stepped over a large puddle. Finally, she arrived at the old well near the rear of the kitchen gardens. The Brodys had long had a pump in their kitchen for water, likely for a few generations, but a well still stood ready to offer water to the kitchen gardens.

Penny had performed this ritual only a handful of times in the past. The very first time had been in the early hours of the New Year just before her sixteenth birthday.

The first maiden to drink from a well, or spring, on New Year's Day, was said to be granted her heart's desire. Some said it must be a wedding, or love, that would come to her before the year was out. That was all well and good, she supposed, but at the moment she worried less for herself and more for Robert.

He deserved every happiness. So, she would drink the water and make a wish for him. Wishes were like prayers anyway. If one put their heart into the effort of the making, there was a better chance of something coming from that heart's desire.

Robert had nearly kissed her. She was certain of it. But why? Had he given up hope on the woman he loved, or only given in to the moment created by the two of them standing so near? The very worst thing Penny could imagine was that Robert had sensed her own longing and acted in order to please *her*.

Penny lowered the bucket into the well slowly, trying to order her thoughts. When she had returned from tending to her burn, a damp cloth wrapped around her injured finger, she had found Robert in the middle of a game of charades. He made eye contact briefly, a reassuring smile on his face, before proceeding to avoid her the rest of the evening. He left shortly after the clock struck midnight, though the party went on for hours more.

The bucket hit the water below with a splash, startling Penny from her thoughts. She gave it a moment to fill, then turned the crank to pull it up again. The cold seeped through the layers of her gown and underthings. Her bare arms prickled. When she left the house, she had not thought to be gone long enough to feel the sting of winter on her skin. Now it was evident she ought to have considered changing more than her slippers for half-boots before making her way to the well.

The edge of the bucket came into view, and Penny grabbed it and pulled the bucket to the rock ledge. Belatedly, she realized she had forgotten to bring a cup or dipper with her. Penny stripped off her mittens and laid them on the edge of the well, then used her bare hands to scoop up the frigid water.

The lantern flickered with a cold breeze; the water in her hand rippled.

Time to make the wish.

Penny took in a deep breath. "I wish for Robert's happiness, that he may find the courage to love someone who will love him in return." Then, she bent to taste the water. It was cold upon her lips and tongue and chilled her throughout to drink it. Water slipped through her fingers to her bodice, making her shiver all the more.

The whole thing had been a foolish waste of her time and made her risk a cold.

Penny grabbed up her mittens and the lamp, and hurried through the mostly sleeping kitchen gardens and back to the house. A warm drop of water fell down her cheek; she brushed it away before it grew cool in the frosty night air.

"I wish Robert loved *me*." The words slipped from between her lips, the first she spoke after the silliness of what she had done struck her. "I wish he knew I loved him." She entered the house, heart heavy.

Aunt Elizabeth waited for her, however, in the guest room set aside for Penny's use. Her aunt already wore her dressing gown and curling papers in her hair. Without a household maid in sight, Penny's own comfort must wait.

"How was it?" Aunt Elizabeth asked, eyes twinkling. "Did you have a vision of your one true love as you drank the water?"

Penny had been too busy thinking about Robert to remember the silliest part of the superstition. "I did not." She sat down and began unlacing her boots. "I made a wish on behalf of another."

"Oh? How intriguing. And selfless. When I was a girl, I wished for true love every time." She laughed quietly to herself, the sort of laugh one indulges in when remembering childhood flights of fancy. "Eventually, I met Matthew, but I do not think all my wishes in the cold had a thing to do with it."

Penny sat up after pulling off one boot. "What is this? If you knew that, why send me traipsing about in the cold?" She shook her boot at her aunt, feigning insult. "That was not a kind thing to do to me, Aunt."

The woman waved her hand to dismiss the pretend affront. "We all need a little bit of whimsy if we are to make it through this life, Penelope Clark. It is not so much the activity that matters as it is the spirit with which you undertake to perform it. You said you made a wish for another, which only proves my point. You put someone before yourself in that moment, which is quite selfless. Tell me. What will you do to make that wish come true?"

Both boots off and tucked beneath the chair where Penny sat, she studied the floor. "I am not certain I can do anything for it, really." She rose and went to her dressing table, sitting before the mirror so she could see all the places in her hair where pins had been tucked and hidden.

"I already tried to help once, and it did not go well." Robert had not at all appreciated her questioning his brothers about his affections.

"Then try again," Aunt Elizabeth said. "We never give up on those we care for, my dear." Aunt Elizabeth rose and came to Penny's side, meeting her gaze in the mirror. "You are an intelligent young lady, full of fire and strength, and you shine brighter than you know."

"Are you going to try to talk me out of becoming a teacher?" Penny asked, one corner of her mouth going upward.

"Did I not just say how I admire your strengths? Though I do believe you would make an excellent instructor to other young ladies, I know your heart does not relish that path." Aunt Elizabeth gently turned Penny to face her, her brown eyes darker than Penny's own, yet alike in shape.

"When your dear parents died," Aunt Elizabeth said quietly, her expression soft, "I vowed I would raise your brothers and you to make them proud. I have done my best, and you made it a joyful responsibility. But I also promised myself, and your dear departed mother, that I would see you happy." She bent and kissed both of Penny's cheeks one after the other. "Penelope." She stared into Penny's eyes with all the love of a mother. "Grant all the wishes you can for others, but do not neglect your own."

Penny said nothing until her aunt turned at the door. "Good night, dear," Aunt Elizabeth said, her cheerful smile returning.

"Good night, Aunt Elizabeth." Penny sat for some time

at her table, not quite meeting her eyes in the reflection of the mirror hanging above it.

Even if she found the courage to work toward her own wish, the other half of the effort would need to be made by Robert. Lifting her gaze at last to stare into the mirror, Penny searched for the answers in her own reflection.

"The worst that could happen is that I lose a friend," she said to herself. "But he will be lost to me anyway should he marry another."

Her aunt saw fire and strength in Penny. Perhaps it was time Penny found it within herself and did something about her wish.

A sneeze shook the window casings of Robert's study. At least, he imagined his sneezes now had the power to make the windows, shutters, and the foundations of his house quake. For three days, he had sneezed without reason or provocation. He also nursed a terrible headache that no amount of peppermint or willow bark tea could cure. He had grown ill the first morning of the New Year, which some might view as a bad omen. Without thought, he had reported for duty to Devon only to be immediately turned out of the house.

Harry Devon acted as all anxious new husbands and expectant fathers, keeping illness as far from his wife and unborn child as possible. "You may return when you stop sneezing," Devon had told him crossly, practically shoving Robert out the door himself. "Take some rest, Ellsworth. We wouldn't want you to miss the masque for a trifling cold, would we?"

The masque would be held the very next day, after most

had lit their bonfires of Christmas greenery and any with yule logs still blazing would put them out. It appeared that Robert would not be free of Devon's edict and, necessarily, would not attend the masque. One of his last chances to see Penny before she left with her aunt and uncle.

A note from the Devons had arrived that morning with his character assignment. He still didn't know what to make of it. "Lord Justice." Was he to dress as a judge with a wig? That certainly didn't appeal to him. Not when he hoped to see Penny there. Hoped to speak to her for a few moments alone. Perhaps even say goodbye. He had already made himself a fool, and he needed no wig to add to it.

A knock at the front door echoed down the corridor. Robert rose slowly to his feet and turned to face the doorway to his study, somewhat confused. Anyone coming from the grand house to speak to him had come to the rear door, at the kitchen, to relay messages from Devon. He wasn't expecting visitors.

The housekeeper's muffled voice drifted back to Robert as she greeted whoever had knocked, and then a loud, booming voice filled the house.

"Ill? My brother, ill? He would never dare. The man works too hard to allow himself even a single day of illness." Of course. It was Samuel.

Robert fell back into his chair and waited.

The study door flew open and Samuel entered, then bowed with a flourish. "Robert, I am informed you are not at all healthy."

Robert glared at Samuel, opened his mouth to retort, when someone else walked into the room behind his brother and offered her curtsy. Penny had come with Samuel.

He practically jumped out of his chair, gaping at her. He hurried to tuck his handkerchief away, then came around the desk to make his bow. "Penny. Welcome." She stood there, in a cream-colored gown and red shawl, a basket in hand, again a picturesque angel while he felt a sickly mess.

"Not a word of welcome for me, eh?" Samuel asked, smirking at Robert from the chair he had already claimed near the fire.

"I cannot say I blame him," Penny said, meeting Robert's gaze with a sympathetic smile. "If he does not feel well, then your yelling will hardly help matters."

From the corner of Robert's eye, he saw Samuel brush that concern aside. "We are come because he is ill. He ought to be thankful."

Robert gave his full attention to Penny. "Is that why you are here? To look in on me?"

She came to his desk and settled the basket she held onto its surface. "That is one reason. I have brought you every concoction that the elder Mrs. Gilbert had available for the treatment of a winter illness. I thought she only enjoyed flower gardens, but she is quite an herbalist." Penny tapped the basket with her hand. "You must be well by tomorrow, Robert."

The sincerity with which she spoke lightened his heart considerably. Penny wanted him at the masque. Had thought of him with enough concern to procure him a basket of treatments and had come with even his horrid brother to pay Robert a visit.

"We have had our masque assignments," Samuel said

suddenly, and Penny immediately glowered at him. "Miss Clark says I am not supposed to tell you what my costume is, but as I hardly think anyone will care—"

"I am not telling mine," Penny interrupted him, narrowing her eyes at Samuel.

With his still-aching head, Robert had no wish to enter into even a playful argument. But Penny. Penny had come to his house and stood in his study. He never thought to invite her to visit, but now that she stood in the middle of the room, he could not imagine her elsewhere.

What did he need to do to make certain she felt welcome? To keep her there as long as possible?

"Would you both care for some refreshment?" Robert asked, somewhat weakly. Did he even have ready refreshments for guests? A bachelor household rarely did. Especially one as small as his own.

Penny took over in her accommodating way. "Robert, you ought to rest. I did not come here to have you wait upon me. If you and Samuel will go into the parlor, I have already asked your housekeeper to lay the fire there. I will take this basket to the kitchen and return with sustenance for all of us." She took up the basket again and gave him an expression that clearly warned him against arguing with her.

Then, she went from the room, head held high, as though she knew precisely what she was about.

Robert stared after her, unable to ascertain through the fog in his head what had happened. But Samuel was on his feet and came to Robert's side, a sly grin on his face. "You heard the orders, Rob. Best do as she says."

In somewhat of a daze, Robert followed his brother out of the room and down the corridor to the drawing room. "How did she come to hear of my illness? Or to be with you?" If he had the energy, he might be jealous. Or at least suspicious of Samuel's influence in the visit.

"Miss Clark visited the Devons again yesterday, then she came straight to my door to inform me that my brother was ill and that I ought to look in on you. Then she invited herself to come with me." Samuel took up a chair near the fire again, then pointed Robert to the couch. "You had best sit there, the better for Miss Clark to lavish attention upon you."

"Lavish—? Do not be ridiculous, Sam." Robert sneezed just as he sat down. "What are you going to be for the masque? I haven't any idea how to dress for my part."

"I am to be the personification of Courage. I'm planning to dress all in red with a sword at my side. What are you?"

Robert groaned. "Justice."

"Ah, then you get a sword, too." Samuel appeared pleased.

"What?" Robert rubbed at his temples with both hands. "I was thinking a wig and robe. Like in a courtroom."

Samuel leaned forward in his chair and lowered his voice. "I happen to know that Miss Clark's costume is a match for yours. Though I will not tell you what it is, respecting her wishes." A wicked gleam appeared in Samuel's eye. "But if you dress in a wig, you will not be fit to be seen with her."

A match. So, Mrs. Devon had assigned Robert and Penny complimentary costumes. Most likely, her husband had put her up to it, given his insinuations that Robert felt more than friendship for Penny. But how did Samuel know anything about it?

"I am open to suggestions," Robert said at last, trying to get comfortable in the corner of the couch. "A sword. Where have I seen Justice holding a sword?"

"In paintings, I would imagine." Samuel stretched his legs out toward the fire, smugly satisfied with himself. "Are you still protesting your feelings for Miss Clark?"

Robert's gaze moved from his brother to the fire, watching as its flames flickered and danced. He was tired of fighting his feelings for his friend. Tired of dwelling on lost dreams. "I have been thinking about what you said on New Year's Eve."

To his brother's credit, Samuel did not immediately crow over the admission. Indeed, he went absolutely still and quiet. Waiting. It was completely unlike him to wait.

Since most of the work he had available in his home was less important and less complicated than his usual labor, Robert had been left without the ability to lose himself in the work of his estate. He had spent many hours dwelling on Penny. Their kiss at the Christmas ball. Running into her in the first place, and her excitement to see him. The near kiss in the hall. And every moment they had spent together in the more distant past.

"I need to do something. Say something." Robert covered his eyes with one hand and released a frustrated breath. "But I cannot decide when, or how, or what to say." Then he sneezed again.

"And you certainly do not want to sneeze in the midst of declaring your love," Samuel put in most unhelpfully. Robert groaned and bent forward, covering his face with both hands. His brother laughed. "I have never seen you in such a state. You are usually calm in moments of crisis."

"Those moments have never involved my heart before," Robert muttered, rubbing his face before resting his chin in his hands. "Penny is in my kitchen at this moment, you realize. The most important place in the house to a woman. She is seeing everything. How poor I am. What I have to offer."

A knock at the door made both brothers stand and turn to face it. Penny appeared, holding the door open for the housekeeper to enter with a large tray. "Here we are," Penny sang out, a cheerful smile upon her face.

"She does not look disappointed to me," Samuel muttered. Robert glared sharply at his brother.

Penny did not seem to notice, as she was directing the housekeeper on where to put the tray, all the while complimenting and thanking the servant in a way that had the middle-aged woman blushing and smiling.

That was good. The staff liked Penny.

When the housekeeper made her curtsy, Penny brought her spoils to the gentlemen. "A mug of broth to Robert," she said, handing a steaming cup to him. "Mrs. Gilbert sent a whole jar over, promising if you had three cups today it would set you to rights." Then, she served Samuel a plate of sandwiches and a cup of steaming cider. She placed another cup of cider at the table nearest Robert. "Yours has a few extra ingredients. Ginger. Echinacea. It ought to help." Finally, she settled herself on the couch next to him, a small plate of sandwiches on her lap. "And now we can enjoy a lovely chat before Robert goes to nap."

That made him pause in lifting the broth to his lips. "Nap? I am not in my dotage, Penny."

"No, but you must rest in order to recover. I have left

instructions on a tea for you to drink that will help you sleep." She fixed him with a look warning him to listen. He was not certain what the consequences would be if he did not, but he had a vague idea he might not like them.

"Very well, Penny. Food and then rest." Then he listened as she spoke, not about anything particularly important. But her voice was soothing in and of itself. The way her tone changed, and words lilted made his whole body relax. She spoke of her visit to the Devons the day before, of how much her aunt had enjoyed renewing her friendship with Mrs. Brody, and of her brothers. Samuel, thankfully, did most of the conversing with Penny. She did not seem to mind, though she made certain to include Robert by sending smiles in his direction now and again.

He admired her profile while she sipped at her cider, finding again how much he adored her. The tip of her nose turned up just slightly, her dimple appeared in one cheek when she smiled widely enough, and her eyelashes fluttered most becomingly when she laughed.

He could not let her go, now that he had her near again.

Robert needed to find a way to tell Penny he loved her and to ask for her love in return. Perhaps he could convince her to wed him. Samuel might be right. The wife of a steward might be better for her than being a teacher. Perhaps she would grow to love him, in time. Fondness could change to love, could it not?

"Robert?" Penny said, speaking his name as though she had already said it several times.

He blinked himself out of his thoughts, realizing he had nearly dozed off. Perhaps he did need that nap after all. "I must apologize. My mind wandered. What were you saying?" He kept his words and expression contrite.

Her eyes softened, and she leaned closer to lay her hand over his. The touch stirred his sleepy thoughts into a hazy desire for action. If only Samuel had fallen asleep or left the room.

"I asked if we ought to take our leave now. I can see without your answer that we must. I do hope you are better tomorrow, Robert." She pressed his hand gently, and he slid his palm over to entangle his fingers with hers. Her eyes widened, very slightly, at the gesture.

"I wish you could stay longer," he said, his voice low and the sentiment for her alone. "When you are near, I feel better than I ever have before." It was not the most charming, nor most sophisticated flirtation. But it was the best his muddled, stuffy head could come up with in the moment.

Penny's cheeks pinkened, but her eyes sparkled at him with delight. "Perhaps a little longer, then." She glanced in Samuel's direction. Somehow, Robert's brother had turned tactful. He had somehow procured a book and sat with it in such a way that it blocked both Penny and Robert from his view. Penny's eyebrows lifted, and Robert grinned.

Carefully, Robert lifted Penny's hand to his lips. Her attention focused on him, her head tilting to one side. He kept his eyes on hers, praying a sneeze would not impede him and watching for any sign of objection. When she made none, he pressed a kiss to the back of her hand. She wasn't wearing gloves. Perhaps she had removed them during her time in the kitchen. Her skin was warm and soft beneath his lips.

Her breathing stilled, her blush deepened. He held her gaze a long moment, then lowered their joined hands to rest between them. "Do you remember the last summer you lived here?" he asked, voice a soft murmur that might not carry to Samuel.

Penny took in a shaky breath before responding. "Of course. I was sixteen. Almost seventeen."

"And I was nearly eighteen." He ran his thumb across her knuckles. "The day before I left for school, by the pond. Do you remember that?"

With maidenly modesty, Penny lowered her eyes to her lap. "We were skipping rocks. I won that contest, you know." She peeked at him from the corner of her eye and he chuckled. Not so modest, then.

"I almost asked you for something that day." She recounted the rocks, but he remembered something different about their time by the pond. He had stood near her, his dearest friend, holding her hand almost as he did now. He had wanted to kiss her and had nearly asked if he might. The words had been upon his lips. But courage had failed him. They were so young. What if she had not felt the same? Perhaps at Christmas, he had told himself, he would try then. When he had released her hand and stepped away, Robert had thought Penny appeared disappointed. Later, he convinced himself he imagined her disappointment altogether.

"That same something," she said, her voice almost a whisper, "that you asked for at the Christmas ball?" Her eyebrows raised, though she did not look at him directly.

Robert reached into his waistcoat pocket with his free hand and withdrew the silver berry. He held it out to her, the berry in the center of his palm. Penny glanced at his hand, then stared at it intently.

"The same thing," he said. "But I had hoped with a different outcome."

Penny raised her gaze slowly to his, and she studied him carefully. "Robert." His name, spoken almost huskily, nearly ended his resolve to hold back. He could lean forward and kiss her, right there, and he felt certain she would allow it.

Samuel cleared his throat from behind his book, and Penny moved away, releasing his hand.

"I think we had better leave," she said, voice raised. "Robert needs his rest." Her cheeks remained bright red, and when she looked at him again, she smiled.

Robert rose to bid them both farewell, sliding the silver holly berry back into his pocket. Samuel rose and dropped the book upon his chair. He gave Robert a somewhat stern look. "You had better recover fully and be at the masque tomorrow."

Penny had already left the room at a swift pace, doubtless to don her winter coat and gloves.

Perhaps she had indeed been disappointed by the pond years back. He did not want to fail her again. "I would not dare miss it," Robert answered, spirits lighter than they had been in a very long time. Something told him he had a chance.

CHAPTER 16

Penny wrapped her knuckles lightly on the door of her aunt and uncle's guestroom. A quiet murmur on the other side sounded like her uncle. She heard her aunt laugh, the sound light and joyful, before Aunt Elizabeth called, "Come in."

Easing the door open enough to slip inside, Penny closed it again quickly behind her. The room her aunt and uncle had been given was larger than Penny's, with a grander bed and wide window. The open curtains allowed the last fading light of day to seep into the room, the glow faint even though it was not yet the dinner hour.

Tonight, all over England, bonfires of green boughs and holly would burn as the last vestiges of the Twelve Days of Christmas were put away. People would celebrate in their villages and homes, even in the larger towns, and on the morrow attend church on the day of Epiphany. In another day or two after that, Penny and her family would return home.

"Penelope, you are absolutely stunning," Uncle

Matthew said, his chest puffing out proudly. "Does not our niece look well, my dear?" He wore a costume that reminded one of a soldier. He was meant to be Admiral Nelson.

Aunt Elizabeth turned from the table where she sat, obviously having completed her *toilette* a short time ago. She wore a tall powdered wig, a white and blue gown, and a small crown of silk flowers. She was to be Victory. She stood and approached her niece; her smile most approving.

"Oh, how lovely. I confess, I was not certain how one playing the part of Mercy must look, but I think you have done beautifully."

Accompanying Penny's costume assignment were the words of Shakespeare:

The quality of mercy is not strained.
It droppeth as the gentle rain from heaven
Upon the place beneath. It is twice blest:
It blesseth him that gives and him that takes.

With some trepidation, she had chosen a simple white gown, the color of innocence, with a blue sash tied about her waist to indicate purity. It was a simple costume, but Mrs. Brody's personal maid had more than made up for it with the painted mask on Penny's face. A swatch of white and blue paint, like a streak smudged on a painting, went from one side of Penny's face to the other, and small white paste gems had been artfully applied at the corners of each eye.

"Mercy sees with Heaven's eyes, miss," the artful maid had told her with a grin.

Blushing under her aunt and uncle's praise, Penny twisted her fingers before her as they knew her to do. "I thank you. I hope I do not disappoint Mrs. Devon in my portrayal. Why she assigned such a role to me, I cannot guess."

Her aunt and uncle exchanged amused smiles. "Did you wish to speak to us before we leave?" her aunt asked.

Penny nodded and came all the way to the center of the room. "I wanted to first thank you both, with my whole heart, for all that you have done for me in the last several years. You have treated my brothers and me as though we are your own children, though you already had your own sons to raise."

Uncle Matthew took Aunt Elizabeth's hand, and neither said a word, though they both appeared curious.

"I wish now to ask you—that is, I would like to know your thoughts on the subject—" She broke off, somewhat nervously, and lowered her eyes to the carpet as she tried to order her thoughts. She had rehearsed her words several times, but they had fled in this crucial moment. She had considered herself brave in showing up to Robert's home unannounced and requiring his health restored. She searched for that bravery again. Without it, her wish would have been made in vain.

"Penelope," Aunt Elizabeth said softly, "you can ask us anything."

When Penny looked up again, her uncle gave an encouraging nod. She took in a shaky breath. "Thank you. I am not certain how best to explain myself. You see, since returning to this place where I grew up, renewing old acquaintances, I have reason to believe there is someone here, an honorable man, who may wish to marry me."

Neither of the Marhams appeared the least surprised

by this news, though Aunt Elizabeth raised one eyebrow knowingly.

Hastening her words, Penny took a step closer to them. "He has said nothing to me. Not yet. But there have been little things. Hints. And I wish to know if either of you would have objections to his suit. He is not a man of land or property, but he is respectable, and could care for me quite well."

"You speak of Mr. Robert Ellsworth," Uncle Matthew said, a gleam in his eye. "Your childhood friend."

Penny gulped away a nervous giggle and nodded firmly. She had not been entirely circumspect in her admiration of him, it would seem. Given that neither of her guardians appeared troubled by the subject, she continued on. "He is a steward. But quite capable of providing for a family."

Aunt Elizabeth stood and approached Penny, holding her hands out. Penny reflexively put her own into her aunt's, waiting for judgment, a word of advice, anything at all.

"Would he make you happy?" Aunt Elizabeth asked, surprising her niece.

Yet Penny knew the answer to that question immediately. "Yes. I love him." She bit her lip after the confession, then laughed somewhat tremulously. "I think I have loved him for as long as I can remember knowing him."

"Then we will see if this young man is intelligent enough to recognize he has won the heart of an angel," Uncle Matthew said, standing beside his wife and laying a hand upon Penny's shoulder. There was something in her uncle's expression that struck her as almost secretive. As though he knew something about the matter that Penny did not. Yet he supported her. Penny could tell that much, and her trembling ceased.

"Come. Let us go to the masque," Aunt Elizabeth said. "Your Mr. Ellsworth will be there tonight, I believe."

"If he has overcome his cold." Penny had not heard from Robert, or even Samuel, as to whether or not the restoratives she had brought did Robert any measure of help. She adjusted the blue sash at her waist and followed her aunt and uncle from the room. There was not a great deal of time left before they must leave. If Robert did not tell her what he wished, if he did not make his intentions known soon, she would return to her uncle's home with a heavy heart.

Of course, Robert could write. If he asked Uncle Matthew for permission. She supposed she could be happy with that much.

But after the way he had kissed her hand, the intent stare filled with warmth and affection, he had not left her mind or heart. Robert had never behaved that way toward her before. Oh, he had come close once, when they were practically children. That day by the pond. Her sixteen-year-old self had thought he would kiss her. She had nursed disappointment for weeks afterward when he had not.

Things were different now. They were both quite grown up.

As she stepped into the carriage, her cloak wrapped tightly around her shoulders, Penny thought back on her New Year's wish. She had wished for Robert's happiness, and she had wished he would love her.

Her breath caused fog to form before her, despite

being inside the carriage. The temperature outside had dropped rapidly, and the rain had ceased at last.

Perhaps that night, if Robert had recovered sufficiently to attend the masque, she would know what the chances were of her wishes coming true.

CHAPTER 17

Robert muttered to himself as he adjusted the sword and the scabbard at his hip. Samuel had brought him the last piece of his costume only an hour before they had to depart for the Devon masque. The sword, though dull, was quite real and thus somewhat heavy. It had belonged to one of their ancestors, a man in the seventeenth century that had left it hanging on the wall of their family manor. Samuel wore one exactly like it, but those were the only similarities in the brothers' costumes.

Peter wore a bow and empty quiver on his back, dressed all in green, as Cupid. God of Love. It seemed strange to have a seventeen-year-old in such a part, but Peter had been happy enough to attend a party with a weapon strapped to him.

As courage, Samuel wore red from head to foot, including a ruby stickpin in his cravat.

But Robert had decided on a subtle depiction of Justice. He wore the sword, of course. Justice always had a staff or sword. He wore black all over: Gloves, shirt, cravat, boots, and a black mask across his face.

The brothers stood in the largest room of the Devon house, a grand corridor with doors open on either side to create more room for the evening's entertainment. While most masques were placed where people acted without inhibition, the Devons had made it clear their evening was about innocent fun for the neighborhood. Thus, there were many participants near Peter's age and even a few younger.

Peter shifted from one foot to the other. "You look more like Death than Justice," he said for the second time to Robert.

"Both are inevitable," Samuel quipped, then nudged his brother. "Look. There is a gaggle of boys and girls your own age. Go show off for them and leave the elders to their own entertainment."

Peter smirked and bowed dramatically. "Of course, grandfathers." Then he skipped out of reach before Samuel could retaliate.

Self-consciously, Robert smoothed his cravat. "He is right. I look like Death. Or a highwayman. But how does one dress like Justice?" He had only ever seen paintings of Justice depicted as a woman holding scales and a sword or a man in Roman armor. As he had no armor, he had thought recalling that judges in the present wore black robes would work as well.

"Forget the pup," Samuel said with an easy shrug. He scratched at his nose just below the mask he wore. "The only opinions that matter are Mrs. Devon's, as she's the hostess—"

"And she seemed approving," Robert noted with some relief.

"—and Miss Clark's, because you are madly in love with her." Samuel's grin would have been aggravating had Robert not accepted the truth of the statement.

Robert rested a hand on the hilt of his sword and returned the grin. "Sam, if you keep saying that out loud, I'll run you through. Dull blade or not."

His elder brother laughed, drawing a few stares in their direction. Samuel's jests no longer ruffled him, but eyes suddenly upon him caused a knot to tie up within. Today would be the day Robert would finally express his love for Penny. Samuel stopped his guffaws and stared over Robert's shoulder with widening eyes. "She's here, Rob."

Before he turned, Robert's heart pounded like a drum in a military parade. When his eyes found her, his mouth fell open in his surprise. Penny stepped into the room on her uncle's arm. She held herself regally, chin level with the ground, half her chestnut hair piled atop her head while the other half fell down her back in ringlets. She had the look of a fairy, or even a princess. Surely only a woman such as she could make the loveliest of storybook creatures come to life. She had never been so enchanting.

Robert had taken four steps toward her before Samuel caught up to him, slowing his progress and hissing, "Close your mouth, Rob. You look like you mean to fall at her feet right in the middle of the room."

Would that be such a terrible thing?

He slowed, pressed his lips together, and nodded his thanks to Samuel. A room full of his friends and neighbors, particularly one in the home of his employer, was not the place to declare himself to the woman he adored. Not so publicly. What had he been thinking?

Samuel stayed beside Robert, which annoyed the younger brother. He had always kept a level head. There was no need for Samuel to act the part of a nursery-maid. Of all nights for the man to hold back, he chose the night he outfitted as courage? It made no sense.

Penny's head turned, and Robert caught her eye. Samuel could take his uncharacteristically cautious atti-tude and go to the blazes. Robert had waited long enough.

With a bow and sweep of his hand, Robert introduced himself. "Good evening, fair lady. I have come to offer my services to you. I am Lord Justice."

Beneath the paint she wore as a mask, her cheeks turned an endearing shade that put him in mind of roses. "My lord." She dropped into a curtsy worthy of St. James's Court. "We know one another, for I am Mercy."

"Ah, the Robber, more like," Samuel interrupted, step-ping almost between Robert and Penny. "Mercy is forever robbing Justice, is she not?"

Penny's lips twitched upward. "I would say that Justice and Mercy are meant to be a pair. My lord," she inclined her head toward Robert, "makes certain there is a cost for wrong-doing, while I determine if there might be some relief for one who is truly repentant."

Samuel's mouth opened but then closed; his eyes narrowed behind his mask. Robert took advantage of the moment and held his arm out to Penny. "As we are meant to be a pair, might I claim the honor of escorting you through the room?"

"Yes, my lord." Penny took his arm, her hand resting

perfectly at the curve of his elbow. Leaning closer than strictly necessary, she whispered, "You cut a dashing figure in black, Robert."

His heart swelled, and he bent his head to return the compliment. "And you are more lovely than ever. Your costume suits you perfectly." He caught her gaze with his and offered a most sincere smile. "Thank you for tending to me. Without your restoratives, I would not be here this evening."

Penny colored prettily. "I am glad I could help. You certainly seem much better this evening." Music began in the next room, and she hesitated before asking, "Have you any desire to dance tonight, Lord Justice?"

"I think I must, my lady," he answered, staring at her intently. Was it too soon to ask her, too foolish to believe she would respond kindly if he laid his heart before her? There were moments in the past two weeks wherein he saw an affection in her eyes as well as fondness in her manner. But if he had read into things too far, his suit would be nothing more than a laughable insult.

He led her into the room where couples had begun to form a line, his courage failing him. Until he stood across from her, and Penny's warm brown eyes met his stare. She lifted one silvery-painted eyebrow at him, then said, "Do you remember when we were children, and we played the wish game?"

His heart practically tripped over itself, just as his feet did when he was called upon to move as he answered. "I remember." They had taken turns and played often with her brothers and his, making wishes and requiring one another to do increasingly foolish things to make them come true. Sometimes it was nothing more than a wish for a biscuit which meant someone had to snatch a biscuit from beneath the cook's nose. Sometimes the wishes were more serious.

"I wish you would tell me what you really think of my costume," Penny said, her voice low as they crossed one another in the dance.

His racing heart sagged in relief. He could make that one come true easily enough. "Granted." He held his hand out and walked forward with her, up the row, bowing to another couple before resuming their stance. "I think you the most beautiful woman I have ever seen." The words were bold, but the truth in them made it easier to speak.

Penny's lips parted, then turned upward. Before she could respond, however, he offered up his wish.

"I wish you had not run away the night of the Christmas ball." When he had kissed her. She had told him to forget the moment, but she surely knew he had not. Not with that tiny silver berry so readily on his person when she had come to call the day before.

"I cannot change that," she answered, her eyelashes lowering. "But I can tell you, if I had the moment again, I would behave differently. I did not think you wished to be caught under the mistletoe with me."

Robert took in a breath of air, his whole frame growing lighter. "I wish there was mistletoe here, now."

After recovering from a moment of what appeared to be delighted surprise, she narrowed her eyes at him, somewhat playfully. "It is not your turn to make a wish."

"Forgive me, Lady Mercy."

"You know I must." She stepped closer to him than was strictly necessary for the next action in the dance, then whispered, "I wish you would kiss me again."

A fierce pounding started in his ears that very nearly put him out of step, but he somehow kept to the rhythm required.

"I cannot tell if you are serious," he admitted, studying the saucy grin she wore. "Or if you are merely being playful." It was a near-relative to the mischievous smile of childhood, but there was more to it now. The smile challenged him to take action as much as it showed her amusement.

Penny tilted her chin upward, her eyes flashing. "Why not both, Robert? You have known me for many years. I am serious in my play, and playful when I am serious."

Oh, how he wanted to scoop her up in his arms that very moment and kiss away that smile until she kissed him in return. It would not do, of course. He could not—

The music stopped.

Of course he could.

Robert took her hand while the other couples arranged themselves for the next dance in the set, leading her out of the line. Without looking back, one hand holding to her and the other resting on the hilt of the sword he wore, Robert wove through the crowds and out into the corridor. Without a word of protest, Penny followed as he took her to the stairs and down to the ground floor.

There he paused, somewhat amazed that no one had stopped them, and that no one stood in the entryway to look askance at them. Not even a footman was in sight.

Penny twined her fingers through his, bringing his attention back to her. When their eyes met, Penny tilted her head toward a pair of closed doors. Another moment and they were through those doors, in a darkened room where only a fire flickered in a hearth to give them light.

He pulled his mask off, then took both her shoulders beneath his hands. "Penny."

Her hands slid onto his shoulders, then behind his neck. "Robert." The firelight reflected in her eyes, dancing merrily. "Are you granting my wish?"

Nothing else needed saying.

Her lips were soft as before, and sweeter. Tired of being careful, overjoyed to have her in his arms, Robert crushed her to him and lost himself in kissing her most thoroughly. Her return kisses—ardent and full of longing —well enough signified she had waited for this moment with as much hope as he. They parted for breath at last, yet he could not refrain from brushing kisses across her forehead, then down the line of her nose, before capturing her lips again.

Penny sighed, a sound of bliss, and Robert finally came to himself. He tipped his forehead to rest against hers, his arms found their way around her waist and his hands locked behind her. "My dearest Penny. You must be able to guess how much I care for you. Will you consider me an alternative to your plans, my love? Will you marry a steward or are you set on becoming a teacher?"

"Oh, Robert." She laughed breathlessly. "I would marry you if you were a clerk, or a footman, or a toll attendant. You are the only man I have ever loved." Then she kissed him, standing on her toes with hands cradling the back of his head. As he was settling into the moment, she abruptly stood back. "You must speak to my uncle—"

"I spoke to him this morning. He gave me his blessing,"

Robert hastily reassured her, chuckling when she frowned at him. "I take it he did not give me away."

"Not at all." She shook her head, then placed one last, abbreviated kiss upon his cheek. "But we had better return to the party before he rescinds that blessing."

Taking her hand in his, Lord Justice escorted Lady Mercy back to the party, quite forgetting his mask. To which no one, not even Samuel or Peter, said a word.

EPILOGUE

DECEMBER 24TH, 1826

Moving on quiet feet, Penny entered Robert's at-home study. A quick glance about showed the chairs both near the fire and behind his desk empty. Pursing her lips, she crossed the corridor to the drawing room. The man could not have simply vanished. Yet he was not sitting upon the couch or in his favorite comfortable chair with a book, either. She turned to leave, but a quiet coo stopped her.

Penny turned back to face the room, puzzled. Robert was not sitting upon the couch, that she could see, but perhaps…

Tiptoeing nearer, Penny peeked over the back of the furniture, and there she found her husband lying upon his back, head upon a cushion, and a small bundle cradled against his chest.

Robert's warm brown eyes met hers in the semi-darkness of the firelight, a drowsy smile upon his face. She came around to kneel beside him, not wishing to disturb the tiny one resting with him. "You sneaked Matthew out of the nursery again," she accused quietly, smoothing back Robert's hair.

His expression turned plaintive. "I could hardly leave him there all alone. On the Eve of Christmas." Robert's smile returned when she leaned forward and kissed him. Then Penny stroked the soft, silky hair of their son. At only eight weeks old, he was the center of their world.

Slowly, Robert sat up, keeping the baby named for her uncle tight against his chest. "Which reminds me. I have a small gift for you."

"Whatever for?" she asked quietly, sitting beside him. Robert stretched one arm behind her, the other remaining wrapped around their baby.

"Because I am your husband, and I can give you gifts anytime I like. But this seems one that is most appropriate to give you tonight, so you may wear it to the ball tomorrow." He kissed her forehead. "Reach into my waistcoat pocket, love."

Penny did and drew out a silver chain. Her lips parted to thank him, but then she saw there was something small dangling from the chain. Frowning, she held the chain up to the light and grasped the small round object in her finger. Then she laughed, though tears pricked at her eyes. "Robert. This isn't the berry, is it?"

"It is." His grin turned sheepish. "I had it turned into a bead. I know it is simple, but I thought you might like to keep that reminder with you. Of last Christmas. Our first kiss. Disastrous though it was."

Penny brushed a tear away as it fell, then hurried to undo the clasp and put her necklace about her throat. "Thank you, Robert." She pressed her palm over the berry and turned to face him, leaning in to kiss him more deeply.

The baby stirred, grumbling softly as babies did whenever they suspected their parents considered putting them down. Penny snuggled into her husband's shoulder and gazed at him, her heart full in a way she never thought possible.

"What is it you wish for?" she asked her husband softly.

"Your happiness," he answered easily, holding her close. "To grant all of your wishes for the rest of my life."

Penny turned to look out the window where snow fell lightly across the pane. "I have everything I could ever wish for, right inside our home, with you."

Between two Christmases, she had found love, become a wife, and a mother. She could not imagine a more perfect life for herself. This life was everything she wished for out in the cold that New Year's morning. Penny's yuletide wish had come true for all of them.

I f you enjoyed this novella, be certain to check out the full series, beginning with *The Social Tutor*, as well Sally Britton's audiobooks on Audible.

You can also keep up with Sally's new publications by joining her newsletter, the sign-up found on her website at AuthorSallyBritton.com

END NOTES

There are many who will debate what was and was not celebrated at Christmas and during Twelfth Night at this period in time. My advice to all is to not hold up a work of fiction, including this one, as an authority on the subject. Do as much research as you can to satisfy your curiosity, and in the end, recognize the spirit in which such a book is written.

For instance, many say Christmas trees were "not a thing" during this time in England, yet we know the royal family had trees, and people loved imitating royalty. There is also mention of a "tree" in the house at this time of year in a Jane Austen letter, and I found a few words about them in newspapers published in 1825, as well as mentions of "Father Christmas."

I like to imagine that many of these traditions were celebrated as they are now, with diversity and each family making the celebration their own.

Merry Christmas, to one and all. However you celebrate this special time of year.

ACKNOWLEDGMENTS

There are always many people to thank upon completing a book, no matter how long or short the story within the covers may be. This time, I want to thank the man who helped me learn that Christmas comes but once a year, yet every day can be Christmas in our hearts - my grandfather, Herbert Clyde Gormley. I miss you every day, Granddad.

Thank you to my dear friend Shaela Kay, who told me early on I was going the wrong way with the story and helped me create something magical instead of something mundane. She also created the beautiful cover of Penny in her red dress - thank you, Shaela.

Thank you to Joanna Barker, Arlem Hawks, Heidi Kimball, and Megan Walker for reading the first chapter (twice) and helping me get the beginning correct.

My fabulous editors, Jenny Proctor and Molly Holt, and my proofreader and assistant, Carri Flores, have helped me weed out errors and oddly phrased sentences. Thank you, ladies!

My handsome husband, Skye, thank you for keeping me supplied with hot chocolate and sweet kisses to inspire me. My loving and supportive children, thank you for giving me time to work and inviting me in to your time to play. I love you all, so much.

ALSO BY SALLY BRITTON

The Inglewood Series:

Book #1, *Rescuing Lord Inglewood*

Book #2, *Discovering Grace*

Book #3, *Saving Miss Everly*

Book #4, *Engaging Sir Isaac*

The Branches of Love Series:

Prequel Novella, *Martha's Patience*

Book #1, *The Social Tutor*

Book #2, *The Gentleman Physician*

Book #3, *His Bluestocking Bride*

Book #4, *The Earl and His Lady*

Book #5, *Miss Devon's Choice*

Book #6, *Courting the Vicar's Daughter*

Book #7, *Penny's Yuletide Wish*

Forever After:

The Captain and Miss Winter

Timeless Romance:

An Evening at Almack's, Regency Collection 12

Entangled Inheritances:

His Unexpected Heiress

Made in the USA
Coppell, TX
01 August 2020